Amy shrieked, and Todd looked where she pointed. "The soap!"

Soap bubbles were spilling over the sides of four washing machines, cascading across the floor in iridescent mounds. By the time they were galvanized into action, Amy and Todd were ankle-deep in bubbles.

"We have to do something!" Amy said. But once she jumped to her feet, she skidded across the floor, landing bottom-side down in the frothy mess.

"Let me help you up," Todd began, but in a moment he was flat on his back next to Amy, and the softness of her body and the shimmering blue of her eyes incited him to action. As he rolled on top of her and lowered his lips to hers, Amy realized there was no escape—and knew she didn't want to, anyway. As she wound her hands into his hair and relaxed against his muscular body, she felt every inch of her body tingle with awareness. She was vividly conscious of the feel of rough denim as their legs tangled together in the soap bubbles, and of the sheer, surprising force of her feelings for this tantalizing, tender—and soaking wet man!

WHAT ARE *LOVESWEPT* ROMANCES?

They are stories of true romance and touching emotion. We believe those two very important ingredients are constants in our highly sensual and very believable stories in the *LOVESWEPT* line. Our goal is to give you, the reader, stories of consistently high quality that may sometimes make you laugh, sometimes make you cry, but are always fresh and creative and contain many delightful surprises within their pages.

Most romance fans read an enormous number of books. Those they truly love, they keep. Others may be traded with friends and soon forgotten. We hope that each *LOVESWEPT* romance will be a treasure—a "keeper." We will always try to publish

LOVE STORIES YOU'LL NEVER FORGET
BY AUTHORS YOU'LL ALWAYS REMEMBER

The Editors

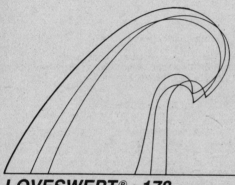

LOVESWEPT® • 178

Peggy Webb
Disturbing the Peace

 BANTAM BOOKS
TORONTO • NEW YORK • LONDON • SYDNEY • AUCKLAND

DISTURBING THE PEACE

A Bantam Book / February 1987

Cover art by George Tsui.

If you would be interested in receiving protective vinyl
covers for your Loveswept books, please write to this address
for information:

Loveswept
Bantam Books
P.O. Box 985
Hicksville, NY 11802

ISBN 0-553-21807-7

Published simultaneously in the United States and Canada

Bantam Books are published by Bantam Books, Inc. Its trademark, consisting of the words "Bantam Books" and the por-
trayal of a rooster, is Registered in U.S. Patent and Trademark
Office and in other countries. Marca Registrada. Bantam
Books, Inc., 666 Fifth Avenue, New York, New York 10103.

PRINTED IN THE UNITED STATES OF AMERICA

O   0 9 8 7 6 5 4 3 2 1

I count myself blessed to have so many wonderful friends. You've shared my laughter, my tears, and my joy. Because your love is my rainbow, my good friends, this book is for you.

One

Amy Logan looked sixteen rather than twenty-six as she darted around her new apartment, blond ponytail flying and freckled nose shining. "Put Herman's spare parts anywhere, Aunt Syl," she said. "I have to take care of this poor little ol' petunia before it languishes away completely." She grabbed a flower box and dragged it to the window. "Don't you worry, Christine," she said to the drooping plant. "We'll have you back in the sunshine in no time flat." Using more grit and spunk than muscle, Amy heaved the flower box onto the windowsill and left it teetering there while she rummaged through a toolbox. "Have you seen my hammer, Aunt Syl?"

Aunt Syl stuck her head out of the closet, where she had been arranging Herman's spare parts. Her lively brown eyes were half hidden by a bright red wig that had gone askew. "Why don't you look in the refrigerator, dear? You're always misplacing things in the refrigerator." Having given that sage bit of advice, she disappeared once more into the closet.

Amy spotted her hammer in a sewing basket. "I've got to get organized," she said for the hundredth time that day. Taking the hammer and a handful of nails, she returned to the window. She pushed the flower box aside to make room for herself and leaned far out the second-story window, her head almost upside down as she searched for a place to anchor her planter. "Ah-ha!" Her hammer made an efficient rat-a-tat against the side of the re-stored Victorian house as she drove the nails home. The grand old two-story building had been reno-vated and divided into eight apartments, four up-stairs and four downstairs. "I hope this racket doesn't bother the neighbors," she said cheerfully to herself between hammer blows.

At last satisfied that her nails would hold, she leaned back inside and carefully lowered the flower box out the window. One side of the box caught securely on the nail, but the other side refused to stay put. Amy and the flower box both hung peril-ously out the window as she struggled to give the petunia a new home.

Suddenly she lost her grip on the heavy flower box and it plummeted to the sidewalk.

"Look out below!" she yelled.

The dark-haired man on the sidewalk side-stepped in the nick of time. The flower box crashed at his feet, spewing potting soil on his expensive leather boots. He glanced quickly upward to see which of his enemies was trying to do him in. Instead of an enemy, he saw a freckled sprite who seemed to be suspended from the window by her toes.

"Is Christine all right?" the sprite asked.

The man looked back down the sidewalk to con-firm what he already knew: he was the only person within yelling distance. "Christine seems to have vanished," he said.

"Christine is my petunia," Amy explained. She was leaning so far out the window that the blood was rushing to her head. She pulled back, but not so far that she couldn't study the man she had almost squashed. His voice was a deep rumble, pleasant but a little formidable. His eyes were as blue as Chesapeake Bay sparkling in the distance. They were the blue of a hundred watercolor seascapes her husband had painted. She closed her eyes for a moment at the thought of Tim Logan. Images crowded her mind—Tim's hair shining golden in the sun, his brown eyes squinted as he studied the changing patterns of autumn leaves on the lake; the intensity of his expression as his brush moved surely across the canvas; his hands slim and gifted, smudged with paint; the stillness of the house after he had gone; the daisies she had planted on the newly turned grave. "I won't think about all that now," she muttered to herself.

"I'm afraid Christine has had an untimely demise." That deep voice brought Amy out of her reverie. Her eyes popped open, and she saw that the man was holding poor Christine by her broken stem. "Fortunately, I escaped the same fate," the man continued.

"I'm sorry."

His eyebrows quirked upward. Amy couldn't tell if he was amused or angry. "Sorry you dropped the flower box or sorry I didn't succumb?"

Even in the bright sunlight she shivered at that voice. It reminded her of drumbeats and horses' pounding hooves and thunderstorms. She smiled at her uncharacteristic flight of fancy and decided that being in the city Edgar Allan Poe had once lived in must have affected her brain. "I'm sorry you were under my window," she said. "And I didn't drop the box. It fell."

"In either case, there is enough evidence to prove that you were responsible." He bit the inside of his cheek to keep from smiling, though he didn't have the slightest notion why he should feel the urge to smile at someone who had almost killed him. He suspected it was the freckles. The sprite in the window reminded him of his favorite beagle puppy. Odd, he mused. He hadn't thought of Frisky in at least fifteen years.

"You sound like a lawyer," she said.

"A judge."

Good grief, she thought. A judge! When she made a mistake, it was always a doozy. She'd probably end up in the Baltimore jail, locked away forever from her wonderful inventions and her kooky Aunt Syl. In her eagerness to smooth matters over, she leaned far out the window. "How can I make amends, your honor?"

He could no longer hold back his smile. That earnest little pixie face and those bare upper arms, nicely rounded and tan from the sun, were enough to make the sphinx smile, he decided. "The name is Todd . . . Todd Cunningham. You can make amends by tapping on my door and warning me the next time you plan to heave a flower box out the window."

Thoughts of jail receded in light of his smile. It was a nice smile, Amy thought. She liked his name too. It had a good, solid ring. A judicial ring. But, of course, none of that mattered. What mattered was that she had been let off the hook. "I did not heave the box." She tried to speak with wounded dignity, but was certain her ponytail spoiled the effect. "And as for warning you, I don't know where you live. Even if I did, I wouldn't tap on your door. Warnings take all the surprise out of life."

"I'll consider myself forewarned, then. I might even run up a flag before sticking my head out my window." He chuckled and shook the dirt off his boots. "It appears that I have the misfortune of being your downstairs neighbor. I hope you don't give wild parties."

"Only on Saturdays and alternate Tuesdays."

"In that case, you'd better introduce yourself so I'll know who to lodge my complaints against." His smile took the bite out of his words.

"Amy Logan." She wiggled her rump and started to inch backward into her apartment. The conversation had gone beyond airborne window boxes. She felt a twinge of guilt, as if she had betrayed the sacred memory of Tim. Fortunately for her, the judge apparently had more important things to do than to stand on Central Avenue talking to a woman who called her petunia Christine.

"I can't say it was nice meeting you, Amy," he said. "Dangerous, perhaps, but not nice." He squared his broad shoulders, a habit he had that signaled dismissal of a matter. "I'll have my butler collect your broken window box and bring it to your apartment."

A butler? she thought, impressed. How did he manage to afford a butler? "That's not necessary. I can do it."

"Somehow, that doesn't reassure me, Amy Logan. I don't trust you with a window box." He nodded in a slight salute. "Good day."

She craned her neck to watch him as he disappeared around the corner.

"What's going on over there?" Aunt Syl asked in her husky, deep-throated voice, surprising in such a birdlike woman.

Amy gave a guilty start and pulled herself back into the apartment. "Nothing."

"That's the longest nothing I've ever seen." Aunt Syl's red wig was now tilted rakishly over one ear. Amy speculated that a small gust of wind would have knocked it off. "I don't think Hortense likes it here," Aunt Syl continued, "and heaven knows what Herman will think when you get him connected." She held a birdcage aloft, and the multicolored Hortense glared at her with a baleful yellow eye.

Amy smiled. Her aunt Syl always spoke of the parrot and Amy's robot as if they were people. Of course, Amy admitted to herself, she sometimes thought of them as people too.

"Give them time, Aunt Syl. They'll adjust. After all, Baltimore isn't so different from Jackson."

Aunt Syl attempted to straighten her wig and succeeded in getting it tangled in her cat's eyeglasses. "I could write a book on the differences." She spoke through the tangle of Dynel hair. "As a matter of fact, I might just do that. I could call it *Murder on Central Avenue*. Did you see the way that concierge looked at us this morning when Hortense called him a fat pigeon?"

"That's in Paris, Aunt Syl." Amy walked across the room and began deftly connecting wires and circuits in her four-foot robot.

"Who's going to Paris?" Aunt Syl, in the way of absentminded mystery writers, had already forgotten what she was talking about. Anyhow, she was still engaged with her willful wig.

"Not who," Amy said. "What. Concierge is French.

Hortense called the building superintendent a fat pigeon. I think Armand ruined your English." She patted the smooth dome of the robot's head. "Time to get to work, Herman." She swiftly pressed instructions into his computer panel. "You can unload the linens."

"Don't let him touch the china. He's hell on china," Aunt Syl warned.

"Give 'em hell, Bulldogs. Give 'em hell." Hortense, who was a great fan of Mississippi State, added a football cheer to the conversation.

"Hush up, Hortense, and let go of my feather boa." Aunt Syl's attempt at anger didn't fool anybody, least of all the arrogant parrot.

Cocking her green head to one side, Hortense admonished Aunt Syl in her best Humphrey Bogart imitation. "Give 'em hell, sweetheart."

"Someday I'm going to sell you to a sailor."

Amy switched Herman on and turned to untangle Aunt Syl. Separating the glasses from the wig was quick work, but a small struggle ensued when she tried to separate Hortense from the feather boa. She tried bribery. "Let go, Hortense, and I'll give you a cracker."

"Batten the hatches," Hortense screamed. She was not to be bribed.

"Let go or I'll pluck your tailfeathers." Aunt Syl said. Her dark eyes were sparkling.

The bird immediately let go and huffed to the corner of her cage.

"I don't know why I put up with her," Aunt Syl remarked as she started toward the combination bed-sitting room that would be hers.

But Amy knew. Hortense had been a gift from Sylvia Street's fifth husband, Armand Depree, the dapper little Frenchman who had showered his adored wife with everything money could buy. But more important, he had lavished upon her the one thing money could not buy—love. The brilliant mistress of mystery, he had called her. Syl had mourned his death in the most practical of ways: she had plunged into her work, creating masterpieces of suspense, books that consistently made the best seller lists, books all dedicated to her beloved Armand.

Amy watched Aunt Syl disappear into her bedroom and wondered if she would ever be able to accept her loss of Tim that way. She had been devastated when her gentle artist husband had gone almost a year ago. She still couldn't bring herself to think of him as dead. It was one of those freak happenings, a tragedy that should have been averted. They had been invited to a friend's house on Pickwick Lake for the weekend. Tim and their friend, Jamie, had taken the boat out. The weather had been balmy and beautiful, not the kind of day that spawned tragedies. Tim had leaned too far out to retrieve a trout line. He had fallen overboard, and his body had been caught in the network of tree roots that fanned under the water in that secluded cove. By the time Jamie had managed to free him, he had drowned.

Amy carefully unpacked one of his watercolors and hung it on the wall. It seemed only last week instead of last year that she had left Tim in the granite silence of the cemetery. She hung another muted watercolor and stood back to admire the paintings, waiting for the familiar sense of his presence that the seascapes always gave her. Nothing happened. She rationalized, telling herself that the hectic week of moving was bound to take its toll. Anyhow, wasn't that why she had moved from

Mississippi to Maryland in the first place, to put the past behind?

She squared her slim shoulders and turned back to her topsy-turvy new apartment. Weaving through the boxes, she walked to a sunny alcove with double windows that overlooked the Chesapeake. "I think I'll set up my workshop here." Twirling around, she spread her arms wide, as if to embrace the sunshine that poured through the windows. "That view is positively inspiring. I already feel an invention coming on. Herman, what do you think of a perpetual popcorn popper?"

The rotund conglomeration of steel and circuits didn't reply. He was too busy stuffing the overflow of linens into the refrigerator.

Amy's vision of the popcorn popper was interrupted by a knock on the door. She opened the door to find a giant of a man standing in the doorway, holding the remains of a flower box . . . her flower box. He must be Todd Cunningham's butler, but she thought he looked more like somebody's lovable bear of a grandfather.

"Miss Logan?" he said. "I'm Justin Oxford. Mr. Cunningham asked me to return this." His voice was a huge boom befitting his size, and his full salt and pepper beard jiggled when he talked.

Amy was enchanted. The only butlers she knew were characters in Aunt Syl's books, and often times they were under suspicion of murder. This jovial giant looked like the kind of man who would take spiders outside rather than squash them.

"Thank you," she said as she took the remnants of her box. "Won't you come in?"

"Not today, Miss Logan. I have a pot roast that needs attention."

As she watched him walk down the hall, she

wondered about the butler. More to the point, she wondered about the man who had a butler. It was a long time before she could get her mind back on the perpetual popcorn popper.

Todd couldn't believe his ears. The raucous sounds of a brass band filled his apartment. He looked at the luminous dial on his watch. Three dammit o'clock. He threw back the covers and pulled on his jeans as the brass band continued to bump and knock above his head. Good Lord, he thought. That fetching woman who threw window boxes hadn't been kidding. She did give loud parties.

He quickly donned his polished boots and a crisp cotton shirt. There was no wasted motion in his movements. He was a man of decision and purpose, a man who needed no adjustment time to come from deep sleep to total alertness. He had to be in court tomorrow—today—and he'd be damned if he'd tolerate that brass band for the rest of the night.

He didn't bother to turn on the lights as he strode through his apartment. He knew the exact location of every polished piece of furniture and every gleaming accessory. At any given time, he could spend a week blindfolded in his orderly apartment and never bump into or trip over a thing. His home was a reflection of his bright, well-organized, analytical mind.

As Todd walked down the hall, he could hear shufflings and muttered curses behind the closed doors of the other apartments. It seemed that Amy Logan's party had disturbed everybody. The halls would soon be crawling with irate people.

He ran up the stairs. There was no need to wonder which apartment was hers. Even if he hadn't known it was the one directly over his, the one vacated two weeks ago by the quiet and orderly Dr. and Mrs. Beeman, he could have picked it out by the racket. As he got closer, he recognized the song "Dixie." It was exactly the kind of song he would have expected Amy Logan to play at her parties. He had detected that soft southern drawl this afternoon. Deep South. Georgia, he guessed, or maybe Alabama or Mississippi.

As he lifted his hand to knock, the door was flung open.

"You're just the man we need." A small blue-veined hand grabbed his wrist. "The music's driving Hortense crazy."

Todd looked down at the petite woman. Tufts of white hair decorated her head like cream puffs and her glasses perched on the end of an aristocratic nose. The network of wrinkles on her parchmentlike skin put her in the category of senior citizen, but her lively dark eyes denied her years. With surprising strength she tugged his arm and pulled him into bedlam.

A gaudy parrot swung from the chandelier; a robot gone mad whizzed round and round, bumping into half-opened boxes; and the aging southern belle with the wild black eyes jumped up and down at his side. "You've got to help us." She had to shout to make herself heard over the blaring music and the squawking parrot.

Todd felt as if he had stepped through the looking glass. Telling himself that his feet were on solid ground, that this was not a crazy nightmare, he glanced around the apartment, searching for the band. It was nowhere to be seen. As a matter of fact, neither were the party guests. Before he had time to reflect on this oddity, Amy Logan appeared in the doorway of a room at the far end of the apartment.

If her entrance had been staged by Hollywood's best director, it couldn't have been more dramatic. She was wearing a bit of pink confection that he fondly recalled as the baby doll pajama. Now he knew why it was called that. Her eyes were enormous and China blue, and her hair fell below her shoulders in a sexy, sleep-tangled mass. She might have been a China doll except that she was backlit by a lamp. The effect removed all doubt that she was a doll. Her small pointed breasts and the soft round curves of her hips were clearly visible through the pajamas. She was pure flesh and blood, as vibrant and desirable as any woman he had ever seen. To his astonishment, he realized he was becoming aroused.

"Where's the party?" he asked. He thought his voice sounded as if it belonged to somebody else, somebody far distant from this enchanted apartment. He blamed his condition on the music, still blasting away.

"The party?" He knew that pink confection had spoken because he saw her lips move. He felt like smiling again. Vaguely, he wondered why she always had that effect on him.

"Yes, the party. Your band woke me up."

"I'm not having a party. That's my bed."

He had never considered himself hard of hearing, but then, he was on the downhill side of thirty-five. Besides that, he had almost been creamed by a flower box. You never knew what kind of damage could result from a trauma like that. "I beg your pardon? Did you say bed?"

"Yes," she said as she breezed into the room, losing her backlight. Todd was sorry. "Something's wrong with it," she continued as she walked over to the alcove, "but I'll fix it." She picked up a large toolbox.

"Wait a minute," Todd said. Now that she had moved, his brain was beginning to function normally. "I'm not clear about the bed. Is the brass band in your bedroom, sitting on your bed?"

"The brass band is my bed." She dodged around a box and captured the robot. She cut off its switches and it whined to a stop. "I'm an inventor, you see," she said to Todd. He didn't see, but he allowed her to continue. "My bed is rigged to play appropriate music—Brahms's 'Lullaby' for sleeping, 'Dixie' for wake-up calls, 'I'm in the Mood for Love' for"—she stopped, obviously flustered—"for other things." He loved the way she blushed. He hadn't seen a genuine blush in years. "I'm afraid my bed got a few wires crossed during the move. The volume is messed up too."

"It certainly is." He was so enamored that he forgot to wonder about her inventions. Besides standing there smiling like an idiot, he felt the strangest compulsion to put his arms around her and pull her head against his shoulder. He wondered what would happen if he did. A loud banging on the door kept him from finding out.

"Oh, dear," the elderly woman said. "Do you think we woke our neighbors?"

For the first time since Amy had entered the room, Todd remembered the perky little woman clutching his arm. "Undoubtedly," he said, and patted her hand. "I know them all. Why don't you let me handle this?"

He gave the older woman's hand a reassuring

pat and walked to the door. He had the uneasy feeling that the explanation he was about to deliver would carry more weight if he were wearing his judicial robes. Even coming from a judge, a bed that played "Dixie" was hard to swallow. As he opened the door to face the crowd, his last thought was that he might lose his reputation and his integrity in one fell swoop.

When the door closed behind him, Aunt Syl turned to Amy. "Oh, my, we're being rescued by a real live hero."

"Not rescued, exactly," Amy said. "And anyway, he's just a neighbor." She rubbed her sweaty palm against her thigh and became aware of her scanty attire. She groaned. What must he have thought? And him a judge. He probably figured she was some flighty southern floozy, trying to seduce him. Carrying the toolbox, she hurried into her bedroom and donned a matching pink robe. A definite improvement, she decided as she pulled the belt tight. She opened her toolbox and set to work repairing her bed. She had to remember that she and Aunt Syl didn't live in their own house anymore, and they had to be considerate of their fellow tenants.

"I liked you better without the robe," Aunt Syl said as she entered the bedroom. "It was much more romantic. Very much like a scene from *Crossfire*." She named one of her many books. "You remember the one." Her eyes sparkled as she entered the dream world of her books. "The heroine is trapped in a Victorian mansion. It's midnight. The hero has to scale a twelve-foot wall to get to her. My, my. Tonight does so put me in mind of that scene."

The talk of romance made Amy irritable. Romance had died with Tim. She stormed from the bedroom to hunt for her needle-nose pliers. "It's three o'clock in the morning, Aunt Syl, not midnight," she said as her aunt followed her. "And that man didn't scale a twelve-foot wall to get here." Heat suffused her body as she remembered the way Todd Cunningham had looked at her. Almost with desire in his eyes. She balled her hands into fists and pressed them against her hot cheeks. She wouldn't think about that right now. "Anyway, he's not a hero," she shouted, partly because of the music but mostly because of frustration. "He's a stuffy old judge."

She whirled as her door clicked shut. Todd was leaning against the doorframe, his perfectly polished boots looking out of place in her upside-down apartment. She wondered how long he had been standing there.

"I think the crowd is pacified," he said. His voice gave nothing away. "Now." He shrugged, the same gesture Amy had noticed that afternoon. "Let's do something about that racket."

"This is where I make my timely exit," Aunt Syl said. She turned to Todd. "I'm Sylvia Street, by the way. Amy's aunt."

"I'm Todd Cunningham," he said, "your downstairs neighbor. Call me Todd."

"Todd." Aunt Syl inclined her head and managed to look dignified in spite of the odd fluffs of white hair. "Now I'll leave so you and my lovely niece can fix the bed."

"Come back here, Aunt Syl," Amy said, but Aunt Syl paid her no attention. Amy pulled her robe tighter as her aunt disappeared into her bedroom.

"That *is* a good idea," Todd said.

"It's a terrible idea."

"Why?"

"Because."

"That answer would never hold up in a court of law."

"This is not a court of law. It's my sitting room."

"I suggest we move on to the bedroom. That singing bed needs some attention."

Amy wondered why she suddenly thought of hot summer nights and tangled sweaty bodies instead of an invention gone awry. "I can give it all the attention it needs." She tossed her long hair back over one shoulder. "Without your help."

"Are you determined to ruin my reputation?"

Her lips parted and she sucked in a sharp breath. The way he said it, with a velvet edge to his voice, made her think of the bed again. "Am I on trial here, your honor?"

"No, Miss Logan. It seems that I am. My neighbors made me promise to take care of that racket." His shrug was eloquent this time, and the way he smiled almost put Amy at ease. "My reputation will be in shreds if they hear me returning to my apartment while your bed is still playing 'Dixie.' You wouldn't want that on your conscience, would you? Especially since you've already tried to kill me today with a flower box."

Amy was beginning to wish she had. Her pulse wasn't supposed to be fluttering like a trapped butterfly. Her palms weren't supposed to be sweaty, and she wasn't supposed to feel giddy.

The no she needed to say to him seemed stuck in her throat. He smiled at her, and she thought his smile was far too wicked for a judge.

"Anyhow," he said, "I need the chance to prove that I'm a hero instead of a stuffy old judge."

"You heard?"

"I did."

"Oh, dear!"

"I think an appropriate redemption would be my admittance to your bedroom."

Of course, she knew what he meant, but that didn't keep other images from leaping to her mind. "Since you put it that way, how can I refuse?" She couldn't believe she had said that. None of this was supposed to be happening. As they entered her bedroom she wondered if tomorrow she would regret this temporary insanity.

Two

She did. When Amy woke up the next morning, the first thing she thought of was the way Todd Cunningham had looked in her bedroom. Big and solid and comforting. A rock to cling to. Somebody to help ease the burden of small day-to-day frustrations. Besides that, he had been cheerful through the entire ordeal of getting her bed to quit playing "Dixie." Not that he knew a thing about electronics. She laughed aloud as she remembered the helpless look on his face when she had handed him a couple of wires. "Can't you just unplug this thing?" he had asked.

She bounced out of bed, singing.

Aunt Syl stuck her head around the door. Today she was wearing a wig of bright yellow corkscrew curls. Her head looked like a giant daffodil. "I haven't heard you sing that song since Tim died. It's pretty."

Amy stopped in mid-phrase. It was true. She used to sing the Jerome Kern torch song, "Along Came Bill," substituting Tim's name in the lyrics. It had been one of his favorite songs. Odd, she mused. She hadn't even been thinking about Tim while she'd been singing. She felt a twinge of guilt, but it was so slight and passed so quickly, it might never have been. "I felt like singing this morning, Aunt Syl. It's a lovely day."

"A day made for love and mystery." Aunt Syl tossed a boa the exact shade of her wig over her shoulder. "Would you come out here for a second? I need you to practice throwing yourself out a twelve-story window."

Amy shucked her pajamas and donned an apple green playsuit. Her aunt's request was not unusual. It was one of the things Amy remembered best about her childhood—helping with her aunt's books. Aunt Syl had been her only family since she was six. While other girls had been playing with dolls, she had been listening to intricate espionage plots or practicing various methods of dying. Maybe that was one of the reasons she had become an inventor, she thought. All that exercise in creative thinking. "We're only on the second floor, not the twelfth," she said as she walked into the sitting room.

"That's all right," Aunt Syl said. "Get in the window and give me a twelve-floor scream."

"Since we're in an apartment now, maybe we should skip the twelve-floor scream. Especially after last night's episode with my bed."

"Fine, dear. Now hop quickly into the window before my muse deserts me."

"Can't I have breakfast first?"

"Dear me, no. Clyde is stuck in chapter six. I've got to do something with him."

"And so you're going to let him jump out the window?"

"Mercy, no. I'm going to let him throw his wife

out the window. Hurry, Amy, before I lose it." "It"
being her inspiration.

Still singing snatches of "Along Came Bill," Amy
cheerfully opened the window and climbed onto
the windowsill. "Head first or legs, Aunt Syl?"

"Head. Clyde's a cad."

Amy leaned far out the window. The morning
sun was sparkling on the Chesapeake. She thought
it looked more like a day for sailing than a day for
dying.

"How's this, Aunt Syl?"

"Lean farther out, dear. There. That's right,"
she said as Any's torso swung upside down. "Open
your mouth as if you're screaming. I want to see
exactly how the veins in your throat look."

Amy was well into her theatrics just as Judge
Todd Cunningham rounded the corner of the
apartment building on his way to court. He was
already late, he thought as he glanced down at his
watch. In all his years of sitting on the bench, he
had never been late. It was that crazy bed. Even
after they had shut it off, he still hadn't been able
to sleep. Or maybe it hadn't been the bed at all.
Visions of China blue eyes and pink baby doll
pajamas kept filling his head. Suddenly he became aware of a body suspended in the air above
him. He halted abruptly.

"Wait," he yelled. "Don't jump. I know last night
was bad, but it wasn't as bad as all that."

Amy gave him a brilliant smile. "Good morning,
Judge. Sleep well?"

Once more Todd had the sensation of stepping
through the looking glass. "I take it you're not
throwing yourself out the window."

"No. I'm practicing dying."

He decided that coming from her, that sounded

logical. "I should be grateful for small favors. You could have been tossing another flower box in my direction."

"I'm helping Aunt Syl add a touch of authenticity to her book. You see, she writes mysteries—"

"Sylvia Street?" Todd wondered why he hadn't made the connection last night, then decided it wasn't surprising. Walking into apartments with parrots on chandeliers and robots running wild and beds playing "Dixie" wasn't an everyday occurrence. "She's one of my favorite writers."

Amy swiveled her head and called inside, "Did you hear that, Aunt Syl? You're one of his favorites."

A head topped by a daffodil-yellow wig appeared at the window. "You're a man of remarkable taste," Aunt Syl said.

Todd laughed. Modesty was not Aunt Syl's long suit, but then, he had suspected that last night. "I try," he said, then watched as she drew her head back into the apartment. He returned his gaze to the woman suspended in midair as he lingered on the sidewalk. Being late had been replaced by being enchanted. "Your cheeks are too rosy," he said.

Amy's hands flew to her face. "My cheeks?"

"Yes. They're too rosy for someone who is dying."

"Don't tell Aunt Syl or she'll let go my legs and run to fetch the powder box."

"Authenticity?"

"Right."

Todd knew that he should be going, but he was reluctant to leave. Amy Logan and her aunt weren't model tenants as the Beemans had been, but they certainly were more interesting. Furthermore, Amy looked equally as good upside down as she did right side up.

"Do you need any help getting back inside?" he asked. He hoped she did. The thought of pulling her in by the legs set off all kinds of fantasies in his head. And he wasn't even a fanciful person. Imagine that. He felt like smiling, so he did.

"No," she answered. "Aunt Syl has a good grip. Besides, I'm not far enough out the window to fall."

"In that case, I'll leave you to your dying. Good day." He turned reluctantly and headed toward district court. Petty misdemeanors would seem bland after seeing Amy Logan "dying" on her windowsill.

Amy smiled as she watched Todd walk away. She didn't know why she was smiling. Maybe it was the sun beaming down on her or the Bay sparkling in the distance. Maybe June was meant for smiling, unlike November, which was meant for grief. She shivered at her last thought, and a chill wind blew over her spirit. Her face suddenly felt damp and clammy as it had that rainy day when Tim had been lowered into the ground.

She struggled to get her torso back through the window. "Pull me up, Aunt Syl."

Aunt Syl tugged on her legs, and she landed with a plop on her unpolished hardwood floor. Seeing her face, Aunt Syl knelt quickly beside her. "My dear! Did I leave you upside down too long? You look like a ghost just walked over your grave."

"It did." Amy jumped to her feet and strode toward the kitchen.

Aunt Syl's feather boa trailed the floor as she followed. "Tim again?"

"I'm afraid so." Amy opened the refrigerator and took out a carton of milk. "I hope we remembered to buy cereal."

"I think you should forget the cereal for a minute and talk."

Amy sighed. Aunt Syl was usually on another planet, but when she decided to come down to earth, she landed with a bang. If she thought Amy should talk, then there was no way the conversation could be avoided. Her aunt was as stubborn as she was eccentric. "I'm listening," Amy said.

"No, you're not. You're just going through the motions." Aunt Syl took the milk from Amy and put her arms around her niece. "Honey, I want you to be happy again."

"Happiness died with Tim."

"Hell's bells and balderdash!"

Amy was startled. In all the time they had talked about this issue, her aunt had never displayed such anger. "He was a wonderful man, Aunt Syl. We had a perfect marriage."

"There's no such thing as a perfect marriage." Aunt Syl spoke with such vehemence that her wig slipped backward. "I ought to know. I've had five."

"Well, I've had one and it's all I want. I have enough beautiful memories to last a lifetime."

"Pooh! Memories don't keep you warm at night. Memories don't take you dancing and buy you champagne." She squeezed Amy's shoulder. "It's time to shut down the shrine and start over."

"What shrine?" Amy asked, but she knew what Aunt Syl was talking about. Photographs of Tim decorated her dressing table; his pipe lay on the bedside table; his watercolors stared down from every wall.

"Indeed!" Aunt Syl crossed the kitchen and pulled down a seascape done in shades of pastel blue. "You can start with this. I've never liked it. Too prissy. Let's put a rowdy Picasso up there. Ah, Picasso. Now there was an artist with *life*."

Amy rescued her watercolor and hung it back on the wall. Her fingertips caressed the painting, tracing the gentle curves of waves lapping against a sandy beach. "This painting has life, Aunt Syl. It also has gentleness and tranquillity."

"What about power and raw sex?"

Amy's back stiffened. "Is this still a discussion of art?"

"It was never a discussion of art." Aunt Syl dramatically swept the boa aside and sat at the kitchen table. "It's a discussion about men. Take Armand, for instance. Ah!" She closed her eyes and threw back her head in ecstasy. "Now, there was a *man*." Her eyes popped open and she pulled her wig back into place. "He could play my body like a virtuoso. And did. Absolutely took control in the bedroom. That's the only time any man has ever controlled me. I had to go through four men before I found the right one."

"I don't intend to go through four men looking for something that I don't want and don't need. I had everything with Tim. *Everything*," she added for emphasis.

"Hah!" There was a whole encyclopedia of disbelief in Aunt Syl's exclamation. "You forget that I see with the eyes and heart of a writer."

"Aunt Syl, I think you should quit trying to see things that aren't there and eat your breakfast."

"I say eat your ice cream while it's still in the cone," she said, paraphrasing her favorite playwright, Thornton Wilder.

Amy was saved further analysis by the entrance of Hortense. The parrot never entered a room unobtrusively. She dive-bombed with raucous squawking and a flurry of bright tailfeathers. "Awk!" She landed on top of the refrigerator. "Batten the hatches and Yankee Doodle Dandy. Shoot to kill, you devil."

"Does Hortense want a cracker?" Aunt Syl asked politely.

"To hell with crackers," Hortense said.

"Someday I'm going to make parrot stew with the old reprobate."

"I'm not holding my breath," Amy said. She was so relieved with the interruption of their discussion that she could have kissed the naughty old bird. Instead, she finished her cereal.

Amy spent the rest of the day unpacking boxes and trying to fit all her belongings into the apartment. She discovered her new apartment was smaller than the little house she and Aunt Syl had shared in Jackson. By the time she had finished arranging Tim's paintings and all the tools for her inventions, her dwelling looked like a cross between an art gallery and a *Star Wars* set.

Aunt Syl had disappeared into her sitting room soon after breakfast, and the constant clackety-clack of the old upright Remington told Amy that her aunt was deeply involved with her muse.

They both fell into their beds, exhausted, at the end of the day. They slept so soundly that neither of them heard the stir of the ceiling fan or the drip of the leaky kitchen faucet. They didn't hear the clatter of the ancient air-conditioning system or the labored groan of the overworked refrigerator. They were deep in the land of dreams and would have stayed there until sunup except for one small thing.

"Help! Murder!" a voice cried in the darkness, rudely jarring Amy and Aunt Syl awake.

Amy sprang from her bed and grabbed her hammer, while Aunt Syl sprang from her bed and grabbed a pair of garden shears. Certain that mayhem was being committed in their very own apartment, they both crept out of their bedrooms and peered into the sitting room.

"Help! Murder!" The voice was so close it chilled Amy's spine. "Murder! Murder! Awk! Batten the hatches."

"Hortense!" they exclaimed simultaneously.

"Murder!" she screamed back. "Give 'em hell, Bulldogs."

Amy dropped her hammer and made a dive for the noisy bird. Hortense immediately flew up to the chandelier, where she continued her ominous warnings.

"There she goes again," Amy said. "Why can't she sleep in her cage like other birds?"

"Well, she's jus—" A loud pounding on their door cut off Aunt Syl's explanation.

Amy looked at Aunt Syl. "Oh, my gosh, the neighbors. Coming!" she yelled as she made a quick detour by her bedroom for a robe.

Aunt Syl tried to coax Hortense down while Amy answered the door.

"What's going on in there?" The man who spoke had thunder in his face as well as his voice. "It sounds like murder."

"It's only a parrot." Amy smiled sweetly, hoping that southern charm would defuse his anger. It didn't work.

"Last night it was a bed. Now it's a bird. A body can't get a decent night's sleep around here since you moved in." The angry man pulled his seersucker robe tighter around his barrel chest.

"Amen to that," another voice chimed in. The speaker's head was poked around the door across the hall, and nothing was visible except her face. She appeared to be in her mid-fifties, and Amy guessed her wrinkles were carefully taped down with adhesive wings. "I dare say everyone on this floor has been disturbed. I for one plan to do something about it." She banged her door shut for emphasis.

"I'm terribly sorry," Amy said to the man who was still standing outside her door. "The move seems to have upset our parrot."

"The move has upset me, young lady. See if you can't keep it quiet for the rest of the night." With that he marched next door to his apartment.

"It seems we've made enemies of our neighbors," Amy told Aunt Syl as she closed the door.

"It'll blow over," Aunt Syl said.

It didn't. Two days later Amy found herself in district court facing petty misdemeanor charges of disturbing the peace.

She sat on a wooden bench near the back of the courtroom beside an unshaven man who reeked of day-old fish bait and stale liquor. A fellow criminal, she thought. Ugh! She tried not breathing, but that didn't work. She scooted as far away from him as possible and slouched down, attempting to make herself inconspicuous. This was her first experience as a criminal. Sweat ran down the side of her face and beneath her collar as she contemplated a fate of swinging from the gallows or wasting away in a cell. She was only vaguely aware of the court proceedings at the front of the room.

Court droned on and on as defendants were called before the judge. Amy shut out everything except her own thoughts and the hum of fans on the vaulted ceiling. The fans did little more than stir the hot air. As morning became afternoon, the courtroom became stifling and the bench uncomfortably hard. Amy began to fidget. She was tired of looking inconspicuous and decided to listen to what was going on up front.

Pushing her damp hair off her forehead, she sat up—and looked straight into the bright blue eyes of Judge Todd Cunningham. She didn't think judges were supposed to look that handsome in their black robes. She also didn't think their eyes were supposed to twinkle. He gave her a solemn wink and continued the case as if nothing had happened. Amy nearly fell off her bench.

She completely forgot about swinging from the gallows as she watched Todd preside. The first thing she noticed was his quick wit. "Walking on water has been done only once, Mr. Tudbury," he told a man who had become inebriated, fallen into the Bay, and created such a racket that the Coast Guard had been called to fish him out. He had been charged with disturbing the peace. "I suggest you stay out of the Bay unless you have a boat," Todd said.

Then she witnessed his compassion as he dealt with a terrified woman whose French poodle had been charged with trespassing in her neighbor's rose garden. "I once had a dog, Mrs. Canfield," Todd said. "I understand how you hate to put Fifi on a leash. But we do have a leash law. Sears is having a sale on leashes this week. Why don't you check them out?"

Amy also noted that Judge Todd Cunningham was stern and formidable when he needed to be. But even as he dealt severely with an insolent lawbreaker, he always retained the quality of caring.

She was almost relaxed by the time her name was called. As she walked toward the judge's bench she noticed that the courtroom was empty except for the bailiff, the judge, the court reporter, and her across-the-hall neighbor, the plaintiff.

"Amy Logan, how do you wish to plead to charges of disturbing the peace?" Todd asked. He tried to keep his expression serious as he gazed down at her. She looked like a naughty child with her sweat-smudged face and the damp curls on her forehead.

She stood on tiptoe and whispered to him, "What will happen if I plead not guilty?"

Todd's mouth quivered at the corners as he tried to keep from grinning. She seemed more like a little girl who had raided the cookie jar than someone who had disturbed the peace. He leaned over the bench and whispered back, "I'll hear both sides of the case and then make a decision."

She bit her lower lip in concentration. "Will it take long?"

"It depends on the people involved."

Amy turned to look at the tight-lipped plaintiff. Even without the adhesive wings of two nights before, her neighbor still looked as if her skin were stretched back toward her ears.

"In that case," she whispered to Todd, "I think I'll plead guilty."

"You'll have to speak up so the court reporter can hear you."

"Guilty, your honor, but not intentionally. It was really Hortense."

Todd couldn't keep from smiling. "Just 'guilty' will do."

"All right. 'Guilty.' " Looking straight into Todd's twinkling eyes, she added in a whisper, "But I don't like it."

He winked at her and Amy felt an enormous sense of relief that her day in court was finally over. Being a criminal made her nervous.

"Can I go now?" she asked.

"Not yet. You have to wait for your sentence."

Her eyes widened. "Jail?"

"No. Merely a fine." He assessed the minimum fine and dismissed court.

"Wait," he said as Amy turned to leave.

"You mean there's more?"

"Yes. Have dinner with me."

"Is that a sentence, Judge?"

"Absolutely."

"I call that abuse of power."

"Guilty as charged."

He stepped down from the bench and took her hand.

"I didn't say yes," she said.

"That's all right. I'm pushy as well as stuffy." They were both smiling as they left the courtroom.

Three

Amy gazed at Todd across the table. It was only dinner, she told herself. After all, a girl had to eat. Besides that, she adored Italian food. Anyhow, he was practically her neighbor, and she did need to learn the town. She was totally unaware of the way her eyes sparkled over her wineglass as she rationalized her situation.

But Todd was not. He couldn't keep from staring at her. "Tell me about yourself, Amy Logan. I know that you throw a mean flower box and put on a great windowsill dying act, but I don't know about your inventions."

"The musical bed is one of my inventions. You remember the bed?"

"How could I forget?" He remembered more than just the bed. He also remembered her in those inflammatory baby doll pajamas.

"My pride and joy is the robot," she went on. "Herman is the prototype. Needless to say, I haven't had much success marketing the bed, but my robots are used extensively in automobile factories in Detroit."

"You look more like an ingenue than an inventor." He smiled. "I'm sure you've heard that before."

She laughed. "Dozens of times. Tell me, what is an inventor supposed to look like?"

"Stooped shoulders, white hair and beard, bifocals."

"Except for the stooped shoulders, you might be describing Santa Claus." She thrust her fork into her huge fresh garden salad. "You don't look like a judge yourself."

"Your turn. What does the typical judge look like?"

"Stooped shoulders, white hair and beard, bifocals." Amy was enjoying the repartee with Todd. Just friendly conversation, she told herself. No disloyalty in that.

He threw back his head and laughed. "Sounds stuffy."

"Do you have to keep reminding me of my stuffy old judge remark?"

He watched her carefully as he said, "I like to remember that remark because it reminds me of what you were wearing when you said it."

Her guard came up immediately. "Don't," she said.

"Don't what? Speak the truth?"

"Don't get personal."

"Why?"

"Because."

He smiled. "That's your favorite reply when you want to avoid answering a question, isn't it?"

"It usually works."

"Not with me. I want to know everything that comes before and after the 'because.' I want to know everything about you." He reached for her hand across the table.

Amy was still for an instant. His hand was big and warm and reassuring, and for a moment she absorbed its strength. Then she carefully slid her hand away from his.

"I don't want emotional entanglements," she said.

Todd noticed her hesitation in removing her hand, saw the brief struggle on her face. A woman running from love, he decided. Why? No need to press the issue now. Give her space. Give her time.

He smiled. "Are you sure you're not a lawyer? 'Emotional entanglements' has an obscure ring to it."

Amy was grateful that he chose to skirt the topic with humor. "My aunt is a writer, remember. While other little girls were learning the ABC's, I was sitting beside her discussing characterization, techniques of plotting, and denouement. Aunt Syl didn't believe in scaling down her conversation to fit a child. Total immersion was the best method of learning, she always said."

"Have you always lived with your aunt?"

"Yes. From the time my parents were killed, when I was six, until I married."

Todd already knew without looking at her hand that she wasn't wearing a ring. Bad marriage? he wondered. Emotional scars? He wanted to know.

"Divorce?" he asked.

"Death." Her blue eyes were suddenly remote. "My husband is dead."

"I'm sorry." He covered her hand in an instinctive gesture of compassion.

This time she didn't feel his warmth. She didn't

feel anything except the numbness that remembering always seemed to bring. "It was a long time ago," she said, but at that moment it still felt like yesterday.

Having said "I'm sorry," Todd was at a loss for words. He looked at her forlorn face and decided she was still grieving. Except for the loss of a grandfather when he was fifteen, he hadn't had much experience with death. The main thing he remembered was that he and his brothers had turned to one another for comfort. Having someone to hold had helped ease the grief.

He wanted to walk around the table and take Amy into his arms, but he sensed that such a gesture would not be welcome. The usually decisive Judge Todd Cunningham was saved the further agony of indecision by the arrival of their food.

He steered the talk to less personal things: he recommended tours of the Inner Harbor attractions—the Baltimore National Aquarium, the U.S. frigate *Constellation*, the World Trade Center, the McCormick Spice Plant. With a sensitivity that was a natural outgrowth of his large and loving family, he sought to make Amy feel at ease.

Amy smiled her gratitude to him. As Todd talked, her linguine and clam sauce began to taste less like cardboard and the remembrances of grief receded. Although she certainly had no intention of taking Aunt Syl's advice, she reasoned that there was no harm in enjoying a good meal with a charming companion. And Todd Cunningham was charming. There was no doubt about it. Besides that, he was her neighbor.

By the time the meal was over, Army was completely relaxed. Once more she was the laughing sprite Todd had first seen dangling from her window.

They left the restaurant in Little Italy and took a water taxi across the harbor. The small motor boat was crowded with homeward-bound diners, and Amy found herself scrunched close to Todd. She didn't protest when he put his arm around her shoulders. It seemed natural and right, there on the moonlit Bay.

She settled comfortably against him. She had the sensation of being in the lee of an enormous rock as she watched the water form a silver plume in the wake of their boat. Baltimore was a pleasant reality, and Jackson seemed very far away.

Todd left Amy at her door with a kiss on the cheek. It was a friendly, neighborly kind of farewell, absolutely nonthreatening and vaguely disappointing. As she entered her apartment, she decided not to think about the disappointment. Pursuing that line of thought could be more disastrous than opening Pandora's box.

Aunt Syl looked up from the book she was reading. "Why didn't you invite the judge in for tea and smooching?"

"That's not funny, Aunt Syl."

Amy kicked off her shoes and padded barefoot to the window. Aunt Syl must have taken up mind reading, she thought. Considering the direction of her own thoughts, "smooching" accurately described what she had in mind. She pressed her face against the windowpane. She didn't understand herself lately. Since moving to Baltimore she had been on an emotional seesaw, swinging between grief and giddiness. She wondered if Chesapeake Bay had anything to do with her state of mind.

"I didn't intend to be funny, my dear," Aunt Syl said. "I simply intended to remind you of life. If being with me all these years has taught you anything, I hope it has taught you to *live*, Amy. Let go of yesterday, because today is all you have."

Aunt Syl rose from her chair and crossed to Amy. Putting her arms around her niece, she rose on tiptoe and kissed her cheek. "Good night, dear."

"Good night, Aunt Syl."

Amy hurried to her bedroom. It scared her when Aunt Syl made sense. She flung off her clothes and ran into the bathroom as if demons were pursuing her. Without waiting for the water to get hot, she stepped into the shower. The cold water stung her face and raised goose bumps on her arms. It was just what she needed to rid herself of ideas like smooching and forgetting the past. She gritted her teeth against the chill. She would never let yesterday go, she decided. It was all she had of Tim.

She turned off the water and groped for a towel. As she wrapped it around herself, she struggled to conjure up Tim's face. His eyes were there, the golden color of an autumn leaf, and his hair, shining in the sun. But the exact shape of his chin was blurry. Had it been round and cheerful or square and determined—like Todd's? No, she thought. She wouldn't let Todd intrude. She tried to force him from her mind and discovered that his blue eyes were superimposing themselves over Tim's brown ones. What was happening to her?

She jumped into bed and pulled the sheet up to her chin as if she were trying to keep her memories from escaping. She must not let them escape. Yesterday lived in her heart. As long as she had yesterday, she had Tim.

The next morning Amy was grouchy and bleary-eyed from lack of sleep. She tried to concentrate on her perpetual popcorn popper, but she kept dropping tools and forgetting what she wanted to do next. On top of that, Aunt Syl's clattering typewriter bothered her. To her overwrought mind, the constant clacking of the keys sounded like a hundred woodpeckers attacking the apartment building.

"I give up," she muttered. "The world will have to wait for my next invention."

She stood and stretched. The afternoon still loomed before her. She realized that she had to do something, anything, to keep busy.

"I'll do the washing," she announced to nobody in particular.

Having made that decision, she scurried around the apartment, snatching up dirty clothes and damp towels. Still not satisfied that she had enough to keep busy, she added a stack of spotless dishtowels to the laundry basket. She was in such a fizz to gather a huge washload that she would have snatched the cover off Hortense's cage if the old bird hadn't stopped her.

"Help! Murder!" yelled the parrot.

"I'm sorry, Hortense. I don't know what came over me."

"Love," intoned the parrot. "Hell's bells, it's love."

"Don't be ridiculous, Hortense. It's no such thing." Amy clapped her hand over her mouth.

"Listen to me. Talking to Hortense as if she's human. She's just a bird. What does she know?"

"Love," Hortense screeched.

"What's all this racket out here?" Aunt Syl asked, emerging from her room. Today her wig was as black as doom. "My muse has hopped a fast plane to St. Thomas. Are you talking to yourself, Amy?"

"Mostly to Hortense," Amy said.

"It's a sure sign." Aunt Syl nodded, and the Cleopatra wig slid down over one ear.

Amy knew better than to ask, but she asked anyway. "A sign of what?"

"Love," screamed Hortense.

"Exactly," said Aunt Syl. "She's just like Poe's raven— uncannily accurate."

"Good grief! I live in a madhouse." Amy rolled her eyes and picked up her laundry basket.

"Where are you going?" Aunt Syl asked.

"To do the wash. One of us has to be sensible." She turned to her robot. "Are you coming, Herman?"

The little robot didn't reply.

"Why don't you turn him on first, Amy?" Aunt Syl asked, smiling with satisfaction.

Amy huffed across the room and punched Herman's computer panel. "Of course, I have to turn him on first. I was just testing you, Aunt Syl."

"Like I said, it's love," Aunt Syl called as Amy and her robot went out the door.

Amy pretended not to hear her.

The laundry room was located in the basement of the apartment house. The stifling heat smote Amy the instant she stepped off the ancient elevator.

"Good heavens," she said. "It's hot enough to melt your insides, Herman."

The robot rolled along behind her, carrying the huge laundry basket.

When they reached the machines, she took the basket and began to divide the wash. Since she had the entire laundry room to herself, she decided that she would use all the machines except one.

"Just in case somebody comes," she said to Herman. "Of course, nobody else is going to be foolish enough to do laundry on this blistering hot Saturday afternoon."

"Except those of us who are desperate."

She whirled around at the sound of that well-remembered voice. As she stared at Todd she almost drowned in those incredible blue eyes. They made her think of the Bay and smooches and living for today.

"Desperate for what?" she asked.

"A clean shirt." Todd walked to one of the machines at the end. "Are you planning to use this one?"

"No. Help yourself. Herman and I have designs on these four." She was glad there would be several washing machines between herself and the judge.

"Herman does laundry?" he said. "I'm impressed."

"Herman does almost anything I program him to do." She bent over the robot and pressed instructions into his panel. "Today, he's going to add the soap."

Why had the temperature in the room risen ten degrees? she wondered. Was it possible that she was going to have a heat stroke, and did it have anything to do with a desperate judge?

"Do you mind if I watch?"

She jumped. She had been so busy with her

own thoughts that she hadn't realized Todd was standing right beside her.

"Of course not. Be my guest."

Her hands fluttered uncertainly over the panel. Had she already instructed Herman to add the soap? She couldn't remember.

"The scientific mind has always fascinated me," Todd said. "I'm afraid my knowledge of robots is gleaned from *Star Wars*."

Amy laughed. "Herman is somewhat more domestic than that."

She stood up and pushed her damp hair back from her face. Todd still had made no move to do his own laundry. She wished he wouldn't stand so close. Being in a water taxi surrounded by other people was one thing, but being in a deserted laundry room was quite another. Her skin felt prickly, and it had nothing to do with the heat.

She reached for her laundry detergent and placed it in Herman's pronged hands.

"Fascinating," Todd said. But he wasn't talking about the robot. He was watching the way Amy's damp T-shirt molded itself to her breasts. "Absolutely fascinating." He decided that doing laundry was going to take on an entirely new dimension now that Amy Logan had moved in. It might even become an erotic experience. Heaven knows, he was having a few erotic fantasies right now.

"Do you always do laundry on Saturday afternoon?" he asked. You sly old reprobate, he added to himself. Why don't you just come out and ask the woman for a date?

"No," Amy replied. "I do laundry on whim."

"Saturday is my laundry day. I hope the whim strikes you on Saturdays."

"The whim rarely strikes on Saturdays."

He returned to the machine at the far end of the row to load his laundry into it. And not a minute too soon, he decided. He had progressed beyond the asking-for-a-date stage and was rapidly moving on to the passionate-kissing stage. Not so fast, Judge, he scolded himself. She's a woman who doesn't want emotional involvement. Remember? Finesse is needed, not bulldozer tactics.

"I thought you had a butler to do your chores," she said.

"Justin doesn't do laundry unless I'm desperate."

Amy was flinging her clothes haphazardly into the machines. She didn't know if she had mixed whites and colors. And she really didn't care. White blouses streaked pink were a small price to pay for finishing this job and getting out of this basement. The prickles on her arms had turned to goose bumps all over her body. It was that white, open-throated knit shirt Todd was wearing. He looked much too bronze and handsome in white. Why didn't he do laundry in his judicial robes? she fumed. It would have been much better for her peace of mind. But, then again, he looked awfully handsome in his robes too.

The laundry room was silent except for the metallic clang of quarters in the machines. Amy and Todd struggled with their separate thoughts as they tried to look as if they were concentrating only on the laundry. The initial spurt of water in the machines sounded like the rush of Niagara in the screaming silence of the basement.

"Well, that's that," Amy said after she had set the last machine in motion. She picked up the book she had brought to read, a gripping novel by Lawrence Sanders, and sat in a chair in the far corner of the room. She tried to concentrate on the words as her robot added soap to the machines. Out of the corner of her eye she noticed that Todd had also brought a book. It looked like a legal tome, enormous and heavy enough to hold down a tent in a tornado. She reread the same paragraph three times and wondered why she had considered this novel gripping and why she kept looking up for a glimpse of an all-too-handsome judge.

Finally Todd slammed his book shut. "This is ridiculous," he said. He stood up and strode purposefully toward her. "Legal precedents lose their attraction when you are in the room, Amy."

She looked up from her book and gasped. "Oh, my Lord!"

"Did I say something wrong?"

"No. The soap."

"The soap?"

"Look at the soap!"

Todd turned around to see soap bubbles spilling from all four of Amy's machines. As they watched, the bubbles cascaded down the sides of the machines and rolled across the floor. They continued to pour from the machine, iridescent and endless. By the time they were galvanized into action, Amy and Todd were ankle-deep in bubbles.

"We have to do something," Amy said. She jumped to her feet and skidded across the floor, landing bottomside down beside the row of washing machines.

"Let me help you up," Todd said.

He waded carefully through the slick bubbles and discovered the hard way that even judges were not exempt from slippery floors. He landed with a whump. And there was Amy, her body soft and desirable beneath his, her China blue eyes wide and questioning. As he lowered his lips to hers he wondered how many kisses had started as good intentions gone astray.

Four

With the bubbles under her and Todd on top of her, Amy was powerless to prevent the kiss. Not that she wanted to, she decided as her mouth opened under Todd's. His lips felt warm and wonderful. She hadn't been kissed in ever so long, and what harm would one kiss do? She wound her arms around his neck and gave herself up wholeheartedly to the kiss.

Todd was surprised by her response. He had meant the kiss to be a brief pleasure, a small yielding to temptation. He had meant merely to sample those tempting lips, to touch lightly and then get on with the business of the soap bubbles; but he was human. As he pressed his body closer to hers, he decided that no man alive could resist Amy Logan, soapy slick and passionate.

His large hands bracketed her face, and his mouth moved over hers, searching, hungering, taking the hot pleasure she offered. His tongue slipped into her willing mouth and created sensations that Amy thought had died with Tim. She felt the quick flush of heat in her loins and the familiar straining of her breasts. It had been so long, she thought, so long. She wound her hands into Todd's hair, crisp hair, wiry hair, not soft like Tim's. She felt herself being hauled against a hard, muscular body, not at all like Tim's. But it felt so good that the fleeting twinge of guilt wilted before it had fully blossomed. What could one little kiss hurt?

Every inch of her felt supercharged and tingly. She was vividly aware of the rough feel of wet denim as their legs tangled together in the soap bubbles. She felt the exact shape and breadth of his chest, the finely toned muscles on either side of an enticing valley smack dab over his heart. His square jaw with just a hint of beard impressed itself upon her memory.

As his kisses seared through her, she was acutely conscious of her surroundings—the hard concrete floor, the slick soap bubbles, the chugging of the washing machines, the constant whirring of her robot. She wanted time to stand still. She wanted to hold on to this moment in this steamy basement. She wanted to wrap the iridescent bubbles around them, insulating them from the outside world.

As she clung to Todd, Amy knew her passion was for this moment and this man. The sheer force of her feelings stunned her. Memories couldn't compete with present reality, and present reality had gone beyond "just one kiss."

She removed her arms from around Todd's neck. She knew that continuing would be foolhardy, continuing would mean endangering her memories.

"The soap," she managed to say.

"Yes. The soap." Todd leaned down and kissed away the last bubble from her face. "I think it should have its own national holiday, like Thanksgiving and the Fourth of July." He was still lying atop her as if he never intended to move.

Not that she wanted him to. But now that the kissing had stopped, her common sense was returning. "Something has to be done," she said.

"I agree. Can you tell your robot to add more soap to the machines? We're running out of bubbles."

"I'm serious."

"I am too. As long as we have bubbles, I can continue kissing you on the grounds of temporary soap insanity."

The way he said it, with his eyebrows quirked upward and a comical smirk on his face, made her laugh. And as long as she could laugh, she knew that she was in no danger from passions gone out of control.

"You crazy judge. I'm sentencing you to thirty minutes at the business end of a mop."

He stood up, pulling her with him. "A small price to pay for my crime. Lead me to the mop." He held her hand tightly as they walked to a utility closet. "Careful, Amy. I won't be responsible for my actions if we fall into the soap again."

His smile was so charming that she ignored the import of his words.

"In that case, your honor, I'll make sure you're not around when I do laundry."

"I thought you did it on whim."

She opened the closet and handed him a mop and a bucket. "How can a woman change her mind if a stuffy old judge is going to hold her to every remark she makes?"

His hand closed over hers on the mop handle, and he seemed in no hurry at all to move along to the cleaning up. In fact, Todd was thoroughly enjoying the moment. He savored Amy's pert little face, and then his gaze raked her from head to toe, admiring her curves, clearly outlined by her wet clothes.

"Stuffy old judges aren't that hard to handle," he said. "Especially by women with China doll eyes." And bodies made in heaven, he added to himself.

Amy's breath caught in her throat as she looked up at him. It was impossible not to see the light in his eyes, impossible not to feel the intensity of his thoughts. She squinched her eyes shut and tried to dredge Tim out of her memory, but he was only a vague shadow. Without a clear picture of the past, she felt like a soldier going to battle unarmored.

Suddenly her eyes flew open. Todd was laughing, a deep-throated boom that drowned out even the loud clanging of the washing machines.

"Do that again," he said.

"What?"

"Squeeze your eyes shut like that. You look exactly like a naughty child who's been caught doing something she shouldn't do."

She pulled her hand away from his and stepped back a pace. It helped, but not much. Being six inches away from him instead of three didn't diminish his charm at all.

"How many naughty children do you know?" she asked.

"Plenty. I have three brothers who were the naughtiest kids on the block."

She laughed. "And I suppose you were an angel?"

"Absolutely. I never did anything more than mastermind our wicked deeds and then stand back to watch my brothers take the punishment when they got caught."

She took another mop from the closet, and they started swabbing the puddles of soapy water off the floor. When the little robot whirled by, she reached over to switch him off.

"I would have sought revenge if I had been your brothers," she said.

"They did. One of my plots involved stealing one of Grandma's zinc tubs and turning it into a boat. We rigged a fine sail with one of Grandpa's union suits."

"A union suit!"

"Yes. That was Jeff's idea. The suit was red, and he said if we got into trouble out on the Chesapeake Bay, the flag could be seen."

Amy was so enchanted with the story that she forgot to mop. What would it have been like to have siblings? she wondered. The way Todd told his story, with laughter in his voice and a sparkle in his eyes, filled a void that she was only vaguely aware of.

"I would love to have seen that boat," she said.

"I still remember it as one of the finest boats that ever sailed the Chesapeake. We spent all afternoon in the Bay. I think we discovered three new countries, located a couple of buried treasures, and whipped a band of pirates who had come to attack Baltimore."

Todd mopped vigorously as he talked. Suddenly, he stopped and looked at Amy. "Hey, you're not mopping. Whose soap is this anyhow?"

"Mine." She started mopping up a puddle. "You're such a good storyteller, I forgot everything except listening. Go ahead. Tell me what happened next."

"You just can't wait to hear about the revenge, can you?"

"No. I have a bloodthirsty streak. It comes from living with a mystery writer."

"Late in the afternoon Jeff sneaked back to the house and asked Grandpa if he could borrow his red union suit. Of course, Grandpa started looking, and Jeff had planted a trail that led straight to me. Mike and Wayne were in on the plan. As soon as Jeff left, they had sent me out in the boat on a secret mission."

"What was the secret mission?"

"They said they had spotted an Indian princess who needed rescuing from pirates. I was to attack by water, and they were to attack by land. They never carried out their part. They were hiding in the bushes when Grandpa spotted his union suit flying above my washtub boat."

"And then what happened?"

"Grandpa always made the punishment fit the crime. He said that since I was so enamored with boats, I could clean and polish his fishing boat."

"I suppose your brothers stood back and gloated?"

"No. They helped me. I pretended to be having so much fun that they naturally begged to pitch in. As a matter of fact, the four of us did have fun. Still do."

The storytelling had made their own chore fun. Amy squeezed the last bit of water into the bucket and surveyed the clean basement floor. "I'm almost sorry there are no more bubbles."

"So am I." Todd gave her a wicked grin. He was thinking of the kiss and not the mopping.

Amy blushed. To cover her confusion, she walked over to her robot and bent to inspect him. "Poor Herman. I'll have to attend to his wet feet."

"Amy." The way Todd said her name, with an edge of command in his voice, made her turn around. "I don't want to leave our relationship to chance. I don't want to depend on whims. Let's chuck this laundry and go on a picnic."

"I don't—"

He interrupted her protest. "It's a beautiful day. We can sail on the Bay."

She laughed. "In a washtub boat?"

"No. I have the real thing—a sailboat that makes you forget everything except the water and the breeze."

Amy was tempted, but she wasn't convinced. A part of her felt that she should battle against this man who kept threatening to obliterate her past. "Herman needs attention. And then, there are all these wet, very soapy clothes." She waved her arms to encompass the four washing machines.

"No problem." With the efficiency of a long-time bachelor, Todd set the machines on "final rinse" and restarted them. Turning around, he grinned at Amy. "There. They'll be done in a minute, then we can throw them in the dryer. You tend to Herman while I pack a picnic. Justin can come down and take out the clothes when they're dry."

"I don't know what to say."

"Say yes."

"I really shouldn't."

"Why not?"

"Because."

"Because is not an acceptable reason." He walked over to her and tipped her face up. "I promise not to bite."

As she looked into his laughing blue eyes, she knew she was losing the battle. "Well . . ."

Todd knew he was winning. He smiled. "I'll even steal a red union suit if it'll make you feel better."

Amy gave in. After all, she thought, what possible harm could come from a man with such a sense of humor? One afternoon in his company wasn't likely to change the direction of her life. She was securely tethered to the past, and one afternoon on the Bay wasn't going to sever that tie.

She felt gay and lighthearted now that her decision was made. Grinning, she discreetly moved her fingers across Herman's computer panel. Without looking, she knew exactly which buttons to punch.

The little robot came to life. He circled around Todd twice, then stopped in front of him. A series of electronic beeps emitted from his comical face as he gave Todd a formal bow.

"Herman thanks you for the invitation," Amy said, "and says that I accept."

"Tell Herman that he's made me a happy man. The next time we go sailing, I'll invite him."

"Don't talk about next time, Todd. Today is a one-shot deal. A sort of celebration for getting all the soap off the floor."

"You never know, Amy. Life is full of good things to celebrate."

"I do my celebrating with Herman." She bent over the robot's computer panel to keep herself from thinking about next times and celebrations with Todd. She flicked a few buttons, and the little robot gave an unwieldy salute. "That's his way of saying good-bye."

Todd leaned down, put his hands on Amy's shoulders, and planted a quick kiss on her cheek. "That's my way of saying I'll pick you up in forty-five minutes."

Amy loved his way of communicating, but she

didn't tell him so. She loved touching. Suddenly she remembered times when she had passed by Tim's easel and had caressed his hair or his cheek or the back of his neck. He was usually so deep in his dream world of art that he merely grunted. Sometimes he would mumble, "Not now, Amy."

She hastily pushed the memory to the back of her mind. She would not let anything tarnish Tim's image. Especially not another man who was becoming more charming by the minute.

"About that sail, Todd. I've changed my mind."

"Why?"

She hesitated. What could she say? That she was afraid of him? Afraid that he would replace Tim's memory? That she wasn't ready to let go of the past? That memories were less threatening than reality? She couldn't say any of those things. An honest confession would open lines of communication that she didn't want opened. She decided to fall back on her stock answer, the one she always gave when she wanted to avoid the truth.

"Because."

Todd immediately wanted to declare that word illegal. Amy had used it to put up barriers between them ever since he had known her. He checked his impatience, reminding himself that she had already made herself abundantly clear. She didn't want emotional entanglements. He smiled ironically. He guessed he should be pleased that he fell into that category. At least he had made some impression. That was better than nothing.

How could he argue with Amy's forlorn little "because"? he wondered. It told him nothing, yet it spoke volumes. He felt defenseless against that word. He shrugged and automatically resorted to the one defense he had—humor.

"It's because of the union suit," he said. "By George, I'm sorry, Amy. Next time I invite you sailing, I'll have a red union suit in my hands."

She smiled with relief and almost changed her mind again. Almost, but not quite.

"That's exactly the reason, Todd. How can I risk sailing on the Bay without a red flag?"

"You're a cautious woman, Amy Logan. I knew that the minute I discovered you had invented a bed that played 'Dixie.' " His smile of genuine mirth took the sting out of his words.

Amy decided a quick retreat was in order. The longer she talked with Todd, the more she wanted to stay. "A bed that needs my attention," she said. "I think I hear it playing my song."

"And which song is that?"

The way he said it, with a soft edge of seduction in his voice, stunned Amy. How could he change so quickly from humor to . . . She wouldn't even let herself think about what he had changed to. She bent over her robot to cover her confusion and quickly punched his buttons. Getting out of the basement was top priority.

"That's a private matter between the inventor and the invention. Good-bye, Todd. Thanks for helping me mop up the soap." She quickly spun around and left the basement, accompanied by her robot.

Todd watched them go. The way Amy had felt in his arms was uppermost in his mind. "That little robot deserves a medal," he said as he turned back to his laundry and tried to squash his disappointment at the canceled sailing date.

Suddenly, he smiled. He strode toward the machines, his disappointment replaced by jubilation. Amy had forgotten her laundry.

Amy was so busy trying to banish Todd from her thoughts that she barely noticed Herman's labored whirring as they rode the elevator up to their floor. The soap bubble business was taking its toll. By the time they had reached the apartment, Herman's electronic parts were grinding and growling like a grizzly bear. Still, Amy paid no heed, all her attention being taken by a certain soapy kiss and the way it had made her feel.

Herman created such a clatter entering the apartment that Aunt Syl rose from her typewriter in alarm. "The saints preserve us," she said. "We're being attacked by lawn mowers."

She opened her door a crack and peered through. Her wig, which was always askew, covered the eye she was using to spy. Impatiently, she pushed the wig aside.

"Ridiculous pompadour," she muttered. "No wonder Marie Antoinette lost her head."

The pile of white curls threatened to topple backward off her head, then settled at an angle that resembled the Leaning Tower of Pisa. With her wig out of the way, Aunt Syl could see her niece. She took in the wet clothes, the flushed cheeks, the heaving chest. Her intense curiosity catapulted her into the room.

"What in the world happened to you?" she asked. "And don't you dare leave out any of the juicy parts."

"I've been doing laundry," Amy said.

"It appears to me you've been in the tub with the laundry."

"Just a small accident. Herman put in too much soap."

"Herman, eh? Since when does that robot do anything you don't tell him to do? I smell a story."

"What you smell is soap. I have to take a shower and change, Aunt Syl." Amy started toward her bedroom, then remembered her robot. "Poor Herman." Turning around, she patted his head and switched him off. "I'll see about you later." Ignoring her aunt, she marched toward her room.

Nothing deterred Aunt Syl, certainly not Amy. She followed her niece into the bedroom, determined to find out what had happened in the laundry room.

"I suppose the soap is the cause of your flushed cheeks," she said.

Remembering the kiss and Todd's remark about soap insanity, Amy flushed even brighter. "It certainly is." She quickly hid her face by pulling her damp shirt over her head.

"Ah-ha!"

"What does that mean, Aunt Syl?" Her voice was muffled by the shirt.

"It means that something happened in the basement." She clapped her hands in delight. "I hope it was a good sex scene. My, I do love a good sex scene."

"Aunt Syl!" Amy dropped her shirt and began to peel off her wet shorts. She tried to look severe, but with unruly blond curls and damp panties and bra, she couldn't pull it off. "You keep confusing fiction with reality. My life is not a book."

"You didn't deny it, so it must be so."

"What?"

"The sex scene."

Amy stripped off her underwear and headed to the shower. She decided it was best to ignore her aunt, especially since she was so close to the truth.

Aunt Syl followed her. When she was hot on the trail of a story, she never gave up.

"Who was the hero? I hope it was that rambunctiously gorgeous judge. Was it the judge, Amy?"

Amy was so startled by her aunt's uncanny accuracy that she forgot to adjust the water. "Ouch!" she yelled as it nearly scalded her feet. "Rambunctiously gorgeous, indeed," she grumbled. "I almost burned myself to a crisp, Aunt Syl. Will you please stop with the Twenty Questions so that I can bathe?"

"Ah-ha!"

"And don't start with the 'ah-has' again." Amy turned the water on full force to drown out her aunt's voice. But even over the increased roar she could still hear Sylvia Street's last comment.

"If I had had a sex scene in the basement with the judge, I wouldn't be up here taking a shower. I'd be in his bed."

The comment triggered all kinds of fancies in Amy's head, most of them X-rated. Amy buried her flaming face in the washcloth.

After she had finished her shower, she was relieved to discover that Aunt Syl had gone back to her work. The steady clackety-clack of the typewriter sounded like a reprieve. Amy didn't want any more discussion about what had happened in the basement. It was already bad enough, she thought, that it had happened at all.

She slipped into cut-off jeans and a pink halter top. It was so hot that she was tempted to wear nothing at all. She walked across the room barefoot, stopping beside her bed, and picked up Tim's pipe. She caressed the smooth stem and the wood bowl, still faintly fragrant from his special blend of tobacco. She sat on the edge of the bed, waiting for the familiar sense of his presence the pipe always evoked. But today nothing happened. She closed her eyes and tried to dredge up Tim's memory, but still nothing happened. To make matters worse, she felt rather foolish, a grown woman sitting on the bed with an old pipe.

She stood up and dropped the pipe into the drawer of the bedside table. As the drawer clicked shut, she felt a small sense of relief.

"Getting rid of the shrine?"

She whirled around at the sound of Aunt Syl's voice. She had been so immersed in her own thoughts she hadn't noticed the typing had stopped.

"Just putting away the pipe," she said.

"I'm glad. Now if you'll just put away some of those pale, lifeless watercolors, we can get on with more productive things."

Amy chose to ignore the remark about her husband's work. She'd done all the self-analysis and delving into the past that she wanted for one day. "As a matter of fact, I do have a new invention in mind."

"Good. You've done nothing but mope and putter since Tim's death. It's about time this apartment was turned upside down by one of your wonderful schemes."

Amy laughed. It *did* feel good to have an invention begging to be tried. "Just wait till I've finished, Aunt Syl." She walked across the room and put her arm around her aunt's shoulders. "You'll love it. It's a perpetual popcorn popper, one designed so that the popcorn addict has an endless supply of freshly popped corn without the bother of having to get up to make a new batch."

Aunt Syl loved popcorn. She was so excited, she

nearly swallowed one of the feathers from her billowing white boa. Amy slapped her on the back as
she coughed up the feather.

"What a team we'll make," Aunt Syl said. "You
with your new invention and me with my fabulous new book. We'll go on tour together—Hollywood, Paris, Rome, London, New Jersey."

"New Jersey?"

"Yes. I've never been to New Jersey. I just thought
I'd throw that in."

"Aunt Syl, have I told you lately how much I love
you?"

"You have, dear, but a body never tires of hearing it." She flung the boa grandly over one shoulder and turned toward her room. "I must get
back to that cad, Clyde."

"Has he thrown his wife out the window yet?"

"Dear me, yes. He's now hatching a plot to do in
his second wife."

Amy was filled with joy as she turned her attention to Herman. Life hadn't felt this good in a
long, long time, she thought. After she had finished making minor repairs to her robot, she
plunged into her new invention. She was so intensely involved with her work that she completely
forgot about her laundry.

The apartment was soon strewn with mysteri-
ous gadgets and filled with the smell of popping
corn. Amy was still barefoot and was whistling
while she worked. Occasionally Aunt Syl came out
to sample the popcorn. They did more sampling
and giggling than work. After two hours they both
had butter smeared on their chins, and Aunt Syl
declared that she had grown to the size of the
Goodyear blimp.

In the midst of all the hilarity, the doorbell
pealed.

"I'll get it," Aunt Syl said. "You get on with your remarkable invention." She flung open the door and peered out from under her Marie Antoinette wig at their unexpected guest. Her eyes sparkled with glee as she recognized Todd Cunningham, holding Amy's laundry and looking every inch the movie star idol. "It's the rambunctiously gorgeous judge," she called.

Amy dropped a screwdriver on her toe. "Ouch!"

Grinning, Todd leaned down and planted a kiss on Aunt Syl's cheek. "How's my favorite mystery writer today?"

"Full of devilment. Why don't you go over there and put some more roses in my niece's cheeks?" She winked at Todd. "And don't let her pretend she's busy. What this house needs is sex." Having made her outrageous speech, Aunt Syl flung her boa across her shoulders and made a grand exit.

Todd didn't try to hide his chuckle. It grew and grew until it was a full-fledged boom of mirth.

"Please, don't encourage her," Amy said. "She's already incorrigible."

"She's like a brisk sea breeze. Invigorating." Todd picked his way through the scattered parts of Amy's latest invention. When he was so close she could see a tiny scar on his chin, he sat down beside her, laundry basket and all.

"There's butter on your chin," he said, and he reached up to wipe it off with his thumbs. His hands lingered to caress her cheeks. "Hmm, nice."

It *was* nice, Amy thought. So nice that she wanted just to sit there in the late afternoon sunshine and bask in the good feel of his touch. So nice that she wanted to shut her eyes and purr. So nice that she wanted to hug his neck. But of course she did none of those things. Instead, she inched away and asked a perfectly dangerous question. At least, she thought in retrospect that it was dangerous, for it led to all sorts of unsettling conversation.

"What are you doing with my laundry?" she asked.

"For starters, I folded it." He picked up the item on top of the basket, which just happened to be her black lace bikinis. His fingers caressed them unconsciously as he held them aloft. "See?"

She gasped. "Those are my panties."

"Undoubtedly." He looked at the label and grinned. "Size five. I'd call that just about perfect."

"I'd call that sneaky." She jerked the panties from his hand and stuffed them into the bottom of the basket. "I don't go around looking at your labels."

"Do you want to see? I don't mind."

"Has everybody gone crazy? It must be this horrible weather. It's fried your brain."

"Rescue me. Take me sailing on the Bay."

"I don't have a washtub."

"But I do." He stood up and picked his way back through her scattered invention. After opening her front door, he reached out into the hall and dragged in a huge zinc tub. A red union suit was attached in rakish splendor to a mop handle.

Amy stared at the unlikely object for a full minute before she burst out laughing.

"How can I resist such an invitation?" she said.

Five

By the time Amy and Todd boarded his sloop, the late afternoon sun had turned the sails to rainbow colors.

"It's magnificent," Amy said.

"Wait till you feel the wind in your face," Todd said. He cast off from the dock and they headed out into the Bay. He let out the sails and they ran with the wind.

Amy caught her breath as she watched the huge sails billow before the wind and felt the surge of the boat. Except for a few sea gulls and some sailboats in the distance, they had the Bay to themselves. A sense of peace settled over her as she looked out across the water. Being this close to the grandeur of nature seemed to put everything else in perspective, she thought. Man's petty tribulations dimmed beside all this beauty and order.

"Have you sailed before, Amy?" Todd asked.

"Twice. Some friends of ours had a sailboat. Not as large as this one, though, and the Ross

Barnett Reservoir seems pale compared to the Chesapeake Bay."

"Everything seems pale compared to the Bay."

She laughed. "Is that an unbiased opinion?"

"No. Totally prejudiced. When a man grows up with something this magnificent, I guess he naturally feels as though it's partially his."

Amy saw the fierce, protective pride in his face. It was another facet of the complex man, a man who was impartial judge, fun-loving prankster, and ardent pursuer. She decided not to think about the ardent pursuer part. It would be best to concentrate on the moment.

"You speak with such intensity," she said. "Do you feel this strongly about everything you consider yours?"

"Yes. The Bay is threatened by pollution. It's a tremendous heritage that I want to see passed on to my children and grandchildren. I'm actively involved in a group to save the Bay. Why don't you join us?"

Amy wondered if the invitation was as casual as it sounded. Probably not. Or was she simply reading meaning into everything he said? As she looked at him, dark hair tousled by the wind and blue eyes squinting into the sun, she suddenly knew the meaning of lust. She was so shocked by her reaction that she stood up abruptly and nearly fell overboard.

Todd's arm snaked out and circled her waist. He pulled her hard against his chest, and she felt as if she had been captured by a dynamo. Her breath whistled out between her teeth, and her whole body seemed to vibrate with the thundering of his heart. She tilted her head to look up, and what she saw made her toes curl. Passion was clearly stamped on his face. His eyes were unnaturally bright, and his jaw was tensed in tight control.

They stood together for a small eternity, scarcely daring to breathe lest the moment end. Amy fantasized that she was a willing captive and he was a pirate about to ravish her. Her whole body yearned forward in anticipation. As her bare legs brushed against his, she could feel the texture of his skin. It was slightly abrasive and intensely masculine. Her legs turned to butter.

She thought about running her hand under his shirt, following that provocative V of dark hair down his chest to see if it felt as springy as it looked. Her mouth went dry.

Todd's fantasies were somewhat more explicit. He thought about lowering her to the deck and covering her slight body with his. He wanted to rip aside the scant halter and taste the nipples he could feel pressing into his chest. He imagined the way her thighs would look in the sunset as he parted them. He could almost feel her satin softness closing around him.

His erotic fantasies were so powerful, there was no disguising his arousal. He didn't try to. He stood boldly in the boat, grateful for every wave that swayed his body against hers.

The sunset painted them red-gold as their separate fantasies held them captive. Only Amy's strongly expressed desire for no involvement kept Todd from taking full advantage of the moment. As much as he wanted her, as much as he could sense that she wanted him, he would not go beyond the bounds she had set.

He loosened his hold and lowered her to a seat. "You'll get used to it." His voice was thick with passion, and he had difficulty moving back to the tiller.

"Used to what?" Amy asked.

She felt as if she had suddenly been deprived of heaven. Against her will, her gaze wandered below the waistband of Todd's cut-off jeans. Her breath came in ragged spurts when she saw the blatant evidence of his desire. She had never known that sailing was such an erotic adventure. She bit her lower lip in an effort to control her erratic breathing and runaway thoughts.

"Used to standing up in a sailboat," he said in answer to her question. "Sometimes it can be tricky." What was even trickier, he thought, was getting his emotions back under control.

"Don't worry about me. I'm an excellent swimmer." She brushed her windswept hair off her forehead. She hadn't meant to snap at him. Just because he had kissed her in the soap, he wasn't going to seize every opportunity to touch her. Was she snappish because she thought he would or because she thought he wouldn't? She didn't seem to know anything anymore. Particularly how to make her heart behave.

"Good swimmers make good sailors," he said. "By the end of the summer you'll be an old pro."

That sounded mighty like future plans to Amy. Although remembering took a great effort, she forced herself to do it. From somewhere in the back of her mind she dragged out her resolve to avoid involvement. She would stick to that resolve even if it killed her. Even if she did feel rather lusty. Or was that lustful? Her face was as pink as her halter from her frustration.

"Don't count on making a sailor of me," she said. "I'll be far too busy this summer."

"Doing what?"

Running from you, she thought. Aloud, she said, "Inventing."

"You'll have time for the antipollution group, I hope. You never did give me an answer on that."

"Goodness, no. I can't control the pollution in my own apartment. How do you expect me to help control the pollution in the Bay?"

Todd grinned. "Is this a brush-off, Amy Logan? If it is, be forewarned. I have the tenacity of a bulldog."

She decided a verbal diversionary tactic was the only safe way to deal with that remark.

"You should be ashamed of yourself! Raised in Poe's burial place and using such a tired old cliché. He's probably rolling in his grave."

"Look who's talking cliché."

Amy laughed. "Aunt Syl would disown me for that one." This was much better than talk of involvement and brush-offs.

"I doubt that. Who would want to disown a beautiful woman with roses in her cheeks?"

Her hands flew to her face. "Roses?"

"Yes. Remember? Your aunt invited me to put them there."

She lowered her hands and carefully folded them in her lap. "I believe I've come sailing with an egotistical man. You didn't put them there, the wind did."

"Try telling that to your Aunt Syl."

"Pay her no mind. She is an incorrigible romantic."

"So am I." He turned the boat so it was facing directly into the wind, and it stopped. He crossed to where Amy was sitting, then took her hand and lifted it to his lips. "You make me feel like a kid again, Amy. Only this time I'm not in a wash-tub boat and the princess is real."

She attempted to lighten the situation with humor. "You're doing better. Poe would approve." So much for failed attempts, she thought. Her hand tingled all the way up to her heart.

Todd turned her hand over and planted a lingering kiss on her palm. "Now I know why southern women are described as having an iron fist in a velvet glove. You're a strong-willed woman, Amy Logan."

He released her hand. Amy was sorry. And that was something she'd have to think about later. Right now, the major problem was getting back to shore without revealing her ever-increasing lust.

"Thank you, Judge Cunningham. Nobody's ever called me strong-willed before. I guess I always considered myself to be quite malleable in Tim—" She stopped. She had almost said, in Tim's hands. For some unknown reason she didn't want Tim to intrude on this sunset interlude.

Todd guessed what she had been going to say. A slight clenching of his jaw was the only indication he gave that it bothered him. He stood abruptly and trimmed the sails to head back toward shore.

"You're strong, Amy. Don't ever forget that." He wanted to add that she was strong enough to forget the past, strong enough to handle a new relationship, but he didn't. As much as he wanted to force the issue, he decided that he'd pushed enough for one day. It was odd, but he'd never thought of impatience as being a part of his character. No wonder he'd remained a bachelor for so long. Women made you do strange things.

Taking the tiller, he set a course into the wind.

*   *   *

Todd didn't know how he had survived the sailing trip with his sanity still intact, but he must have. He was leaving Amy at her apartment with nothing more than a safe kiss on the cheek. After she had closed the door, he rammed his fists into his pockets so hard he almost ripped the seams. To make matters worse, he could hear her inside, humming "Red Sails in the Sunset." As he stalked down the stairs to his apartment he decided there ought to be a law against women with China blue eyes wearing pink halter tops. Furthermore, shapely suntanned legs should be banned from Baltimore. Contributing to the delinquency of a judge. That was what Amy Logan had been doing.

He banged into his apartment with unnecessary vigor.

"Is that you, sir?" Justin appeared in the doorway leading to the kitchen.

"Yes."

"I've prepared beef tips marinated in wine."

"I would have preferred halter tips marinated in sunset."

"I beg your pardon?"

"Never mind me, Justin. I'm suffering from an overdose of sun."

"The heat is getting to us all, sir."

Todd sat in his favorite chair by a window overlooking the Bay. He could have found the chair with his eyes closed. It was always stationed precisely beside that window, turned just so to afford the best possible view. He was still for a moment, looking in the direction of the now-darkened Bay, imagining the peaceful scene that he knew was there.

"Justin, tomorrow go up to Miss Logan's apartment and bring down that washtub."

If Todd had turned around, he would have seen Justin struggling to keep from laughing aloud.

"Is this something new you're adding to the decor, sir?"

"No. It's just something I borrowed from Grandpa Tuck. I'll return it later."

"Shall I serve dinner now?"

Todd, who was usually punctual to a fault, did the unprecedented; he postponed his meal. "In a while. I have to think about . . ." He hesitated before doing something else completely foreign to his nature: he was not concise and articulate. "Things," he finished.

He would have been astounded if he had seen Justin shaking with laughter once he reached the safety of the kitchen. The butler laughed so hard he had to wipe tears from his eyes. He did a gleeful jig as he put the beef tips under the warmer. "It's about time cupid paid us a visit," he said.

Upstairs in her apartment, Amy was undergoing the same struggle as Todd. She had come to her senses midway through "Red Sails in the Sunset."

"Too much sea air," she muttered.

"Hell's bells, it's love," squawked Hortense.

Startled, Amy glanced toward the chandelier. The gaudy bird was not there.

"Love!" Hortense continued. "Love makes the world go 'round. Awk! Give 'em hell, Bulldogs."

Amy followed the sound of the parrot's voice. Hortense was hiding behind the plastic dome of the perpetual popcorn popper.

"Come out from there, you naughty bird." Amy shooed Hortense away. "Why don't you ever stay in your cage? Love, indeed! Everybody around here thinks he's an expert on the subject."

"Talking to the bird again, dear?" Aunt Syl emerged from her room. "My, my. You must have had a lovely sail with that gorgeous judge. Just look at the roses in your cheeks."

"It's the wind." But it wasn't the wind at all, and she knew it. It was the touch of a man's hand, the feel of his lips on hers. She hurried toward her invention so that she could pretend to be hard at work and not have to carry on this conversation. On her way across the cluttered room she stubbed her toe on a wrench and fell backward into the laundry basket.

"Watch your step, dear," Aunt Syl said. "One of these days one of us is going to have to get organized."

They both blanched at the word. Organization was as remote to them as Outer Mongolia.

"Maybe next year," Amy said. "Right now all I want to do is work awhile." She was still sitting in the laundry basket. Somehow it seemed appropriate. This whole business with Todd had started with the laundry; it might as well end with it too.

"Well, don't forget to eat, dear. I think there's a bit of lettuce in the refrigerator. It's a mite wilted around the edges, but it'll do for a salad. I'm off for a rendezvous with Clark Gable."

Amy smiled. Anyone who didn't know Sylvia Street would have thought her senile. "An old movie on TV?"

"A movie I rented for the VCR. My, my, that man can set the old juices flowing." She started toward her room, then turned for one last word. "But having spent the afternoon with the sexy judge, I'm sure you know all about that, don't you, dear? Good ni-ight."

Amy scrunched down in the laundry and pretended she hadn't heard. She glared at the bird, who chose to waddle after her owner rather than fly.

"Don't you say a word," Amy warned.

Hortense stared back at Amy and said again, "Love."

Amy supposed the old bird wouldn't have bothered her if she hadn't been so uncannily accurate. What she was feeling right now was so close to love, it scared her to death. Love wasn't supposed to happen in Baltimore. Love had died in Mississippi. The granite marker was evidence.

Amy plucked her black bikini panties from the laundry basket and tried to recall times she had used such frivolous underwear to seduce her husband. The past was dim. All she could call to mind was the way Todd had looked with the wind at his back.

"This is absurd," she said. "I just won't think about it right now." Then, feeling rather foolish, she got up from the laundry basket and went to the kitchen to fix a wilted salad.

The next day Amy was still making a valiant effort not to think about Todd. As long as she was working on her invention, she managed nicely to put him from her mind. But when she ran into a hitch with the popcorn popper and had to stop work, he invaded her. She felt limp and flushed and curiously happy. Although Baltimore was again hot enough to bake bread on the sidewalk, Amy knew the heat wasn't responsible for her condition.

She glanced at one of her husband's paintings and, for the first time, she saw them objectively. They were good in a subdued sort of way, but they lacked a certain depth and vitality. They were tranquil, but somehow lifeless.

"I will not do this," she said fiercely. She searched for her sandals among the clutter. One was under a plastic dome and the other was in her toolbox. Quickly she put them on. "I'm taking Herman for a walk, Aunt Syl," she yelled.

The rackety Remington stopped and Aunt Syl poked her head out the door. "Pick up some food on your way back, unless you want to eat birdseed. I'm going to the outdoor concert at the Inner Harbor tonight." She started to pull her head back in, then changed her mind. "Why are you taking Herman out, anyway?"

"He needs a workout so I can be sure he's functioning properly since the laundry room fiasco."

"That's not what I call it."

"I don't want to hear what you call it, Aunt Syl." Amy hurried from the apartment with her robot.

Herman didn't seem to have suffered any damage, she decided as they exited the elevator and went outside into the sunshine.

Patting his domed head, she said, "I'm proud of you, Herman. I think I've made you indestructible."

Amy and her indestructible robot strolled up Central Avenue. Knowing that Herman always created a sensation, she had programmed him to salute and wave at intervals. The curious people who stopped to watch their progress were certain the robot was waving especially to them. Occasionally, Amy stopped to chat and to demonstrate her robot. She created more goodwill in one afternoon than most ambassadors create in a month.

"I love this city, don't you?" she said to her robot as they entered a tree-shaded residential street. "The people are all so friendly."

They continued their stroll, blissfully unaware that fate awaited them just around the corner. Amy stopped to admire a rose garden, and Herman got ahead of her. A large yellow tomcat leaped down from a fence just as the robot rounded the corner. The cat arched his back and reached out to claw the robot's leg. Herman was not deterred. He continued to roll forward. Furthermore, his metal legs did more damage to the cat than the cat's claws did to him.

Amy caught up with them just in time to see Herman step on the cat's tail, sending the terrified cat scampering up a tree. He scratched and clawed and yowled his way to safety, startling a family of blue jays. They promptly dive-bombed from the tree and landed smack-dab in the middle of the Ladies' Auxiliary summer picnic being hosted on the other side of the fence by Mrs. Matilda Hildenbrand. The screaming and squawking resulting from the unexpected meeting of the jays and the Ladies' Auxiliary could be heard half a block away.

If Amy had been Hortense, she would have used a choice word or two. Instead, she brought Herman to a halt with the remote control and clambered over the fence to see how she could make amends. The fence was tall and she was short, but fear hastened her on, for the screaming on the other side had risen an octave. In her haste she tore a rent in her blue jean skirt and lost the topmost button on her blouse.

She teetered uncertainly on the top of the fence, seeing no way to get down except by jumping. She shut her eyes and jumped, landing in the middle of bedlam. She opened her eyes, then wished she hadn't. Three screaming matrons were waving their arms, trying to shoo away the screeching jays, while another woman was standing atop a swaying glider, batting her Panama hat in the air and yelling, "Get out of here, you birds!"

A woman, whom Amy later learned to be Mrs. Matilda Hildenbrand, descended on her.

"Young lady, are you responsible for this?"

Amy looked up at the distressed woman and wanted to laugh. She was accustomed to mayhem and knew that laughter sometimes relieved the tension. But this poor woman was obviously not in a jovial mood.

Amy stood up and brushed grass off her skirt. "I'm afraid Herman scared your cat, and the cat scared the birds—"

"I don't have a cat," Mrs. Hildenbrand interrupted. "That obnoxious creature belongs next door. In all my sixty"—she stopped to correct herself—"fifty-five years I've never seen anything like this. We may never get Marlene off the glider."

"I'm terribly sorry," Amy said. "My robot and I—"

"Robot! Did you say *robot*? What's this world coming to? A body can't have a decent summer picnic without being invaded by technology. Microwaves were bad enough—turning the canapés to rubber—but robots are simply unthinkable."

"Herman is really quite nice. As a matter of fact, I'll bring him inside and he can help clean up this mess. It's the least I can do, since he's the one who scared the cat."

Mrs. Hildenbrand pursed her lips and stretched her long neck so that she was looking down her skinny nose at Amy. "Young lady, what's your name?"

"Amy Logan."

"Well, Miss Amy Logan, I wouldn't have that robot in my yard if my hair was on fire and he was holding the only bucket of water in Baltimore. You've caused enough damage for one day. But rest assured that Mrs. Matilda Hildenbrand will see that justice is done. I'll see you in court!"

Amy made a hasty retreat. The only glimmer of sunshine left in her day was that she spied a gate behind the oak tree. At least she wouldn't have to climb back over the fence. Grateful for small favors, she went through the gate and rejoined Herman.

Her steps dragged as she headed back to her apartment. She was totally unaware of the grand old city, washed gold by the lowering afternoon sun, and of the people who smiled as they passed by. All she could think of was the ill-fated summer picnic and the threat of another day in court. What would happen to her? she wondered. This was her second offense. Would she go to jail this time? Would Todd be her judge? Would knowing a judge help?

By the time Amy reached her building, she had imagined all sorts of horrors. Her shoulders sagged as she pushed open the heavy, ornate door. She felt the burden of her plight, and it was doubly heavy because she had no one to share it with. Not even Aunt Syl.

She pushed the elevator button and shuddered at the thought of going upstairs to her empty apartment. Why hadn't she gone to the concert with her aunt? Why hadn't she stayed home and baked a cake? Why hadn't she made any number of other choices?

As the elevator doors swung open in front of her, Amy suddenly knew that she was not going upstairs. Taking her little robot, she walked down the hall, scanning the doors for the name she sought. There it was—the apartment directly below hers. Just seeing the name, Todd Cunningham, printed in brass and looking every bit as solid as the man himself, gave her comfort.

Taking a deep breath, she punched the doorbell. She heard the echo in the apartment and waited. There was no sound. She punched the bell again.

"Please be there," she said. "I need somebody to talk to."

"I'm glad you came to me," she heard Todd say behind her. She whirled around, her face lighting at the sight of him. He looked so solid and good standing there in the hall that she almost threw her arms around his neck.

"I didn't really . . ." she began. "It was just that . . . You see, Herman caused . . ." She stopped, not sure what to say to him now that she had impulsively sought him out. She didn't want him to get the wrong impression. As she stood uncertainly in the hall, a tear slid down her cheek. Her need welled up inside her, so overwhelming that impressions didn't matter anymore. She flung herself into his arms and sobbed against his shoulder. "Oh, Todd . . . Mrs. Matilda Hildenbrand is going to take me to coo-uurrt." The last word was a wail as she released all her pent-up anxiety.

At that moment Todd wanted to bow down and kiss Mrs. Matilda Hildenbrand's feet. He hugged

Amy close, rubbing her back and making soothing noises. With his chin resting on her soft hair, he smiled and smiled and smiled. If all his days in court could end this way, he thought he would be the happiest man in Baltimore. Probably the happiest man in the whole world.

He stood in the hall holding her, not daring to move for fear of breaking the magic spell. The front of his shirt was damp from her tears. She clung to him, burrowing her face against his chest, and he thought his heart was going to explode with joy.

Reaching carefully into his pocket with one hand, he backed against his door, fumbled with the lock, and backed into his apartment, still holding Amy. He kicked the door shut with his foot.

She lifted her tear-stained face. "I'm sorry. I don't know why I'm carrying on like this. It's not as if I'll be hanged or anything." Her brave smile was tremulous around the edges.

"There's nothing to be sorry about. You need a friend, and I'm here." He smiled down at her. "And no, you won't be hanged. My guess is that Mrs. Matilda Hildenbrand will charge you with disturbing the peace. It will be just like the last time except easier because you'll know what to expect."

"Is that all?"

"No. That's not all. I'll be there." He chucked her under the chin. "How can anything bad happen to a China doll like you when I'm around?"

Now that the burden of the unknown had been lifted, Amy became aware that she was still in Todd's arms. She was also aware of how good those arms felt. What surprised her even more was that she didn't feel the tiniest glimmer of guilt. There was no sense of betrayal, no urgency to preserve Tim's memory, no desperate need to cling to the past. As a matter of fact, she felt no need to leave the shelter of Todd's arms, so she stayed.

Her smile was as free as sunshine on a summer's day as she looked up at him. "With my penchant for getting into trouble, perhaps I should have a whistle to summon you."

"You don't need a whistle. I'll always be there for you."

She laughed. "Like the Force?"

"I think you've been seeing too many Star Wars movies." He grinned. "No. Like a good friend." And more, too, if she'd let him, he added to himself.

"I'll remember that." Since there no longer seemed to be any real reason for being in his arms, she pulled away reluctantly. "I have to be going."

"Why?"

"Because I left poor Herman in the hall . . ."

"Bring him in."

". . . and it's almost time for dinner."

"You're invited to stay for dinner."

"Aunt Syl might come in and not know where I am."

"We'll call upstairs and tell her."

"And—" She clapped her hand over her mouth. "Oh, my gosh, I forgot to buy food. There's nothing to eat in my apartment except birdseed."

"You wouldn't want to deprive Hortense. Stay and have dinner with me."

"Is that an invitation or just an act of charity?"

"An invitation." And an act of passion, he added silently.

"In that case, I accept."

"I have to warn you. This is Justin's night off. Does the guest of honor object to kitchen duty?"

"I'm a whiz with wilted lettuce, but I don't do dishes."

"Neither do I."

"Herman does."

"Then by all means, let's invite him to dinner." Todd swept open his front door, and Amy brought her little robot inside. The three of them moved through the immaculate apartment to the kitchen.

"Are you sure he can handle the dishes?" Todd asked as he began to unload the makings of a Chinese dinner from the refrigerator.

"He does dishes with the same skill that he handles laundry."

Grinning, Todd walked to a cabinet and began rummaging around. "I'm sure it's here somewhere," he muttered.

"What?"

"The soap." He turned and held a box of soap powder aloft. "We don't want Herman to run out of soap, do we?"

"Is that a trick question?"

"No. But it's definitely a loaded one."

"You are a pushy judge. I knew that the first time I saw you."

"Guilty as charged."

"Criminals don't get off lightly in this court-room," she warned.

Their easy repartee had brought roses to Amy's cheeks again. She was having so much fun, she forgot about her impending day in court. She forgot about the tear in her skirt and Mrs. Matilda

Hildenbrand and the forever silence of death. She forgot everything except the moment. It was too precious to waste. No matter what tomorrow would bring, she was going to live this moment to the hilt.

"Sentence me, Judge Amy Logan," Todd said.

"One hour of hard labor at the stove. I'm starving."

"Then you landed on the right doorstep. My Chinese cuisine is unsurpassed in Baltimore."

Six

After bragging about his Chinese cooking, Todd was determined to outdo himself with the meal, but Amy kept distracting him in unexpected ways. He handed her a fork and told her to stir-fry the mushrooms. Unfortunately for his peace of mind, she stirred with such enthusiasm that she jiggled and bounced. It was not a motion conducive to helping him keep his mind on cooking, especially since the top button on her blouse was gone and he kept getting provocative glimpses of her cleavage. He wiped his sweaty brow on a dishtowel and tried to concentrate on the egg rolls, but it was useless. Egg rolls lost their appeal beside Amy's evident charms.

She turned and smiled at him. "Are these ready?"

"If they were any more ready, they would explode."

"Do mushrooms explode?"

"What?"

"I said, do mushrooms explode?"

"Not lately."

"You're the Chinese food expert, not I. If you say

they're ready, I guess I'll take them up. Do you have a bowl?"

"Do they need one?"

"Todd! Are you listening to me? You seem a million miles away."

He recovered enough to take his gaze off the front of her blouse. "I'm not as far away as you think. What did you say about the mushrooms?"

"We're past the mushrooms. I asked about a bowl."

"In the cabinet."

When she turned around and stretched on tiptoe to rummage in the cabinet, he realized the jiggling couldn't hold a candle to this new distraction. The rent in the back of Amy's skirt partially revealed the sassiest rump clad in pink silk he had ever seen. He stared openly at her, wishing for a sudden whirlwind to come through his kitchen and rip the skirt some more. As he admired this new view, he squeezed the poor hapless egg rolls until they lost their water chestnuts. The chestnuts clinked onto the countertop unnoticed while Todd considered whether he should get five years or fifteen for what he was thinking.

Amy turned around with her bowl, depriving Todd of his wonderful view, and caught him squeezing the egg rolls.

"Aren't you supposed to seal those egg wrappers together gently?" she asked.

"No. This makes them pink."

"Pink?"

"Did I say pink? I meant stick."

She innocently swung her back to him again, and executed another jiggle as she dumped mushrooms into the bowl. Todd wondered how he had ever managed to prepare Chinese dinners without this fantastic scenery. He wondered what Amy would say if he asked her to become a permanent addition to his kitchen—torn skirt, pink panties, and all. He thought his culinary skills—not to mention his fantasies—might take on new dimensions.

That he finally managed to put the meal together was a remarkable feat. That he managed to sit across the table from her and actually carry on a conversation while eating was an even greater accomplishment. Particularly since he wanted to whisk her off to a desert island somewhere. He figured he could spend about six years getting to know each breast and another six discovering the wonders underneath those pink silk panties.

He lost track of the conversation so frequently that he feared Amy would read his mind and take flight, but she was completely carefree now that the burden of court had been lifted. A herd of elephants could have marched through the dining room and she wouldn't have cared.

Over the egg rolls they talked of music and sailing and beds that sing. Over the sweet-and-sour shrimp they talked of his brothers and grandparents and her aunt Syl. Over the green tea they created a blueprint for changing Washington, D.C., then laughed at their audacity as they began to devise a plan to change the world. By the time they got to the fortune cookies, they both felt that deepening respect that comes from getting to know someone you already admire.

"I haven't enjoyed a meal this much since I arrived in Baltimore," Amy said. "Thank you."

"You're welcome. Was it the food or the company?"

"Both." She laughed. "Can I amend my stuffy

judge remark? I want to make that 'audacious judge.' "

"Careful. I don't share my fortune cookies with women who misbehave."

She made a show of lowering her eyes and folding her hands in her lap. "Decorum is my middle name."

"In that case, have a cookie."

He passed the basket to her. Her hand hovered over it as she pondered her selection.

"I don't know whether the big ones have the best fortunes, or if the small ones are better," she mused aloud. "What do you think?"

He loved watching her. He loved the way she bit her lower lip in concentration and the way she tipped her head so that her hair spilled away from that small, determined jaw.

"It's a momentous decision," he said. "I think you should take your time deciding . . . two or three days perhaps."

Her head shot up. There was no mistaking his intention.

"Todd." It was a soft plea, a useless denial of the tension between them.

His chair hit the floor as he jumped up and strode around the table. He put his hands on her shoulders and lifted her from the chair. She turned as naturally in his arms as if she were meant to be there.

"I've been wanting to do this all evening," he said as he lowered his lips to hers.

The magic began. The kiss didn't pretend to be a gentle tasting as the one in the soap had been. It was an explosion of passions too long denied. It was fireworks and drum rolls and bombs bursting in air. It was lightning and whirlwinds and summer storms. And it took Amy completely by surprise. She had known that she was attracted to Todd, but she had never suspected this kind of overwhelming desire.

She was astounded as the wild need built within her. She hadn't known she possessed such primitive passions. Nothing in her past had prepared her for such an onslaught of feelings. Never had she felt as though she were reaching out to touch the sun.

She wound her hands in his hair—that wonderful soldier hair, crisp and commanding—and pressed herself as close as she could to his chest. At that moment, she thought it was the most magnificent, the most reassuring chest in the whole world. And she didn't ever want to leave it.

With their lips still melted together, Todd backed Amy out of the kitchen and into his den. A passion almost out of control guided him toward the sofa. Amy felt the soft cushions press into the backs of her legs. Another moment, and she knew she would be past the point of no return. She struggled briefly with her feelings. She didn't want to give up the magic, she didn't want to let go of the joy, but could she go one step further? She made a small sound of indecision against his lips.

He slackened his hold just as an enormous grandfather clock chimed the hour. It was the clock chime that broke the spell. She eased out of his arms.

"No." The word was barely a whisper.

Todd looked down at her. "Amy?"

"I can't . . . The clock . . ."

"I'm going to chop that thing up into firewood." With a great effort he reined in his fierce emotions. "What about the clock, Amy?"

"It reminded me of what time does. It takes away. Things happen."

She stopped, confused. The words had just come pouring out. She dared not think of what they meant. Lifting her chin, she looked up at him and smiled. "The clock reminded me that I forgot all about Aunt Syl. She's probably up there in that empty apartment wondering where in the world I am."

"If I know your aunt, she's so busy being delightfully eccentric that she's hardly given it a thought."

"I must go."

"Stay."

"I can't."

"Why?"

"Because."

"Damn."

"What did you say?"

"Damn. I'm beginning to hate that word."

"I do too. Don't let Hortense hear you say it. Her language is bad enough already."

"Not *that* word. Your word—because."

She laughed. "It serves the purpose."

"What purpose?"

"Subterfuge." She reached her hand toward him, then changed her mind. How could she touch him, she wondered, and not stay? At this point, touching was too dangerous. She lowered her hand and clenched it behind her back. "Good-bye, Todd. Thanks for the dinner."

"Then you're really leaving?"

"Yes."

"Go quickly while I can still let you."

She spun around and fairly flew from the room.

She was halfway to the front door before she remembered Herman.

"I forgot my robot."

Todd had recovered sufficiently to remember that he was the host and she was a departing guest. He followed her into the kitchen, where she was bent over Herman's computer panel.

"Amy."

She jumped as if she had been shot. "Don't ask me again to stay," she said without turning around.

"I just wanted to say thank you for being my dinner guest."

She turned and smiled. "You're welcome, and thank you for being my rescuer." With one hand she switched on the little robot, then headed for the front door.

Todd watched her until she was almost across the room, then he grabbed the cookie basket and followed her.

"Amy."

She turned slowly toward him, thinking that if he called her name one more time in his magnificent iron-velvet voice, her legs would never carry her out the door.

"Yes?"

"You forgot your fortune cookie."

He reached for her hand and pressed a fat cookie into it. "You'll never know your future until you read this. He held on to her hand until the air fairly crackled between them.

She withdrew her hand and laughed somewhat breathlessly. "With all the uncertainty in Washington, everybody should have a fortune cookie. Thanks." She flew out the door, her cheeks flushed and her eyes unusually bright.

"Hurry, Herman," she said as she ran toward the elevator. "Aunt Syl will be in a panic over our disappearance." As she pressed the elevator button, she knew that Aunt Syl had nothing to do with her flight. The reason for her haste was Judge Todd Cunningham, standing behind his solid door in his immaculate apartment, beckoning her to come into his orderly life. She clenched her fist, fighting temptation. She squeezed so hard that her fortune cookie disintegrated.

As the crumbs dropped to the floor, she felt the slip of paper in her hand.

"Who believes in fortunes?" she muttered. She started to throw the paper down, then changed her mind. "Littering." Bending over, she carefully picked the cookie crumbs off the floor and dropped them into her skirt pocket. But she still clutched the fortune in her hand.

Herman caught up with her just as the elevator door swung open, and they went upstairs to her apartment.

"I'm home, Aunt Syl," she called when she opened the front door.

Aunt Syl walked out of the kitchen. "Have you been somewhere, dear?"

Amy dropped the small slip of paper into her toolbox as she walked toward her aunt. She bent over and kissed the wrinkled cheek. "I can see that you missed me."

Aunt Syl swept through the apartment in her bright blue caftan and waved her hands in the air as she talked. "Did you know that Justin is an expert on weapons?"

"Justin?"

"Todd's butler."

"I know. But how did you?"

"I haven't had a chance to tell you, have I, dear?" With her caftan billowing around her and her Cleopatra wig securely on her head for once, she sat in a chair. "He came to get the tub while you and Herman were gone. We started talking." She laughed. "He's a delightful man. Witty, articulate, absolutely charming. Anyway, we started talking and ended up going to the concert together. He's promised to be my weapons consultant for the book I'm working on."

"Aunt Syl, you amaze me."

"Why?"

"Because you collect friends the way some people collect coins. You seem to—" Amy stopped, at a loss for words.

"Embrace life is the phrase you're seeking, Amy."

"I suppose."

Aunt Syl laughed. "It's catching." She stood up and headed toward her bedroom. "Good night, dear. It's been a longer day than I thought, and for once in my life I'm going to admit that I'm tired."

"Good night, Aunt Syl." Amy had never heard her aunt say she was tired. She watched Aunt Syl leave the room and noticed that she was actually quite fragile-looking. The thought alarmed her. Aunt Syl was so vital that she had never thought of her as being old. "Please, God, not my Aunt Syl," she whispered.

Amy dressed quickly for bed and pulled the covers up under her chin. Never mind that the air conditioner was laboring almost uselessly and that the apartment was hot and muggy. Covering up was an old childhood habit, a shutting out of all the bad things that could befall a person. She squeezed her eyes shut.

"I just won't think about it," she said aloud. Aunt Syl looking fragile and Todd looking virile became jumbled in her mind. "Not any of it," she muttered. "I won't think about any of it."

And with those defiant words, she tried to sleep.

Considering the restless night, Amy felt better in the morning than she had imagined she would. She bounced out of bed, humming. The first thing she did after dressing was check on Aunt Syl. She pushed open the bedroom door and tiptoed in. The bed was empty.

"Aunt Syl," she called softly.

"Down here, dear." The old woman was stretched out on the floor.

Amy rushed across the room and knelt beside her. "Aunt Syl! Don't move. I'll call an ambulance."

"Why? Has somebody died?" Aunt Syl grunted as she sat up. "Three," she said.

"Three what? Aunt Syl, what's the matter with you?"

"Three sit-ups, Amy." Aunt Syl got up stiffly and sat on the edge of the bed. "I can do only three sit-ups."

"You were doing *sit-ups*? I thought you had had a heart attack."

"For goodness' sake, Amy. When I get ready to die, I'll do it in style, not on the floor."

Amy's laugh was shaky as she sat down on the bed and hugged her aunt. "Nobody's going to die," she whispered into the sparse, cream-puff hair. "You're too tough to die."

"Darned right." Aunt Syl pulled away and patted her niece's face. "Unless you squeeze me to death. What has you in such a dither this morning?"

"You scared me last night with your talk of feeling tired. You're never tired."

"Yes, I am, Amy, I just rarely admit it. When a person gets to be my age, he has to focus on the positive. If I let myself think about being old and tired, I'd be sitting useless somewhere, wrapped in a shawl and watching time pass by. I don't watch life from the sidelines, Amy. I get in the game."

"Stay in the game, Aunt Syl. I need you."

"I intend to." She smoothed Amy's hair back from her forehead. "You don't need me as much as you think, Amy. You're strong and you just don't know it."

Amy didn't want to think about being strong without Aunt Syl. She stood up.

"Neither one of us will be strong if we sit on the bed all day. What do you want for breakfast, Aunt Syl?"

"I'll have some bran muffins later, dear. Right now, Clyde, the incredible cad, is calling me."

Amy left Aunt Syl with her incredible cad and hurried toward the kitchen. On her way through the sitting room she paused to look at her walls.

"There are too many pictures in here," she said. She took one of Tim's watercolors down and stood back to view the empty space. "That's better."

She reached for another, and another. The more paintings she took down, the better she felt. The stack of them grew into a huge pile. She dragged a box from the closet and carefully packed them away. When she had shut the closet door on the paintings, she viewed her walls with satisfaction. One seascape, her favorite, remained on the wall. It was a view of the Gulf coast, a blue-green wash of water, sparkling in the sun. In the foreground was a shrimp boat with an old man leaning over the rails, pulling in a net.

Amy suddenly realized that the picture was her favorite because of the fisherman. Tim rarely put people in his paintings, but he had captured the old man perfectly—his shock of white hair, the lively eyes peering out of a brown, wizened face. The old man's zest for living seemed to leap from the canvas.

Her moment of epiphany came as she studied the painting. Her marriage had not been perfect. She had been clinging to an exalted version of the past. In a quiet way, her marriage had been good; but something had been missing. This painting held the key. Amy loved and enjoyed people; Tim had not. His frequent withdrawal into the world of art had not been dedication but rather escape. Even their intimate relationship reflected his failure to relate well to people.

Amy felt a sense of relief as she turned away from the painting and went into the kitchen. It was good not to have the burden of perpetuating a shrine. She had finally put Tim's death into perspective.

As she poured milk onto her cereal she felt such a stirring of energy that she could hardly wait to start her day. The first thing she was going to do was organize her workroom.

After breakfast she tackled the project with enthusiasm. Aunt Syl's typewriter, clacking away in the next room, made a perky accompaniment to her task. She stacked small sheets of metal and separated computer parts. She collected scattered tools off the floor. For thirty minutes she was an efficient whirlwind, then she glanced down at her toolbox. The small slip of paper was still there. It was the fortune she had never read.

Her multicolored peasant skirt flared around her as she sat on the floor and picked up the paper.

"One plus one equals happiness," she read aloud. "How obscure," she muttered, wadding the paper into a tiny ball. She dropped it into the bottom of her toolbox. She started to turn away, but the paper seemed to stare accusingly up at her. Reaching into the box, she retrieved the fortune and smoothed it open. Her fingernail traced the words as she thought of one plus one. Todd. Todd and Amy. Sailing into the sunset. Laughing over the Chinese meal. Embracing in the soap. Happiness.

"Maybe there's more to these Chinese fortunes than people think," she said to nobody in particular.

She carefully folded the paper, tucked it into her skirt pocket, and got on with the business of housecleaning. The more she cleaned, the more clutter she created. She discovered that organizing required boxes, which had to be fetched from the closet. And boxes required shelves, which she didn't have. She stopped amid her accumulated clutter and started to build a shelf.

The hammering sent Hortense into a pout on top of the chandelier and drowned out the sound of Aunt Syl's typewriter. As she worked, Amy felt a song coming on, and of course she had to sing loudly in order to be heard over the noise of the hammer.

In the middle of the enthusiastic carpentry and the rousing song, Todd appeared in the hall with an empty cup. He had come to borrow sugar. You sly old devil, he had thought as he climbed the stairs. Borrow sugar, indeed!

He stood in the hallway with his hand poised over Amy's doorbell. He could hear the words of her song clearly over the sound of hammering. A slow smile spread across his face as he lowered his hand and stood there listening. He wouldn't have pressed that doorbell for all the tea in China. It might have meant missing the song. Amy was belting out a Fats Waller blues song—"Honeysuckle Rose."

When she got to the part about not buying sugar but simply touching her cup, he decided that fate must have smiled on him today. He tapped his cup lightly in his hand as he listened to the rest of the song. He had never considered himself an egotistical man, but he naturally assumed he was the sugar she intended to stir up. And that was fine with him. Better than fine. It was absolutely the best plan he had heard all day. Better than borrowing sugar. Yessir, he mused, he'd go right in there and let Amy stir his sugar up.

The song came to a crashing conclusion, crashing because it sounded to Todd as if she had dropped the hammer on the floor. He pressed the bell in alarm as another loud crash sounded through the door.

"Come in," a voice called.

Todd needed no further invitation. He pushed open the door as Hortense continued her tirade. "Come in, come in, fool. Give 'em hell, Bulldogs. Batten the hatches. Come in."

Todd completely ignored the bird. All his attention was focused on Amy. She was standing in the middle of what looked like the wreckage from a tornado, looking down at her hammer and the remains of a shelf.

"Oh, dear," she said as she looked up at him. "It broke."

Todd picked his way across the clutter and gently took a nail from her hand. "Carpentry is not your strong point."

They plunged as naturally into the conversation as if Todd had been expected. Since the cup was no longer needed as an excuse, he placed it on an upturned box and reached down to pick up the hammer.

"What are you trying to build?" he asked. "I'm a pretty good hand at this."

"Where are your robes?"

"You lost me."

"I thought judges had to wear robes in court."

"I'm not in court today. Sometimes judges get days off."

"Shelves."

"I beg your pardon?" As usual, he felt as if he had stepped through Alice's looking glass. He couldn't decide whether it was the topsy-turvy apartment or the enchanting woman. Probably both.

"I'm building shelves," she explained. "I'm getting my workroom organized."

He suppressed a laugh as he viewed the disorder that she called organization.

"So I see." But, of course, he didn't. Organization to him meant polished floors and neatly arranged furniture and everything in its place. "Perhaps I can help."

"Do you have a magic wand?"

"No."

"Then I don't know whether you can help or not. I don't seem to be very good at organizing things."

"That's okay. Just think what a dull world this would be if everybody had the same talents."

"I can't grow plants, either. Look what happened to poor Christine."

Todd smiled as he remembered the airborne window box and the wilted petunia.

"If you want plants, I'll have Justin bring you a window box full. He has a green thumb."

"That will be wonderful! I want blue ones and pink ones and red ones and yellow ones. I want to look out my window and think of a rainbow. I want—" She stopped in the midst of her enthusiastic response and stared at him. "Why?"

"Why what?"

"Why would you have Justin do that for me?"

Todd considered his answer carefully before he spoke. He couldn't tell her that he loved her. Not yet. He wasn't even sure of that himself. He didn't want to tell her that it was just a neighborly gesture, for that certainly wouldn't be the truth. He decided to choose the middle ground.

"Because I like you, Amy Logan, and I'm happy that you're my upstairs neighbor. You're a delightful woman, and if a window box promotes my cause, then I'll give you a rainbow of flowers."

Amy didn't ask what his cause was. She wasn't sure she wanted to know. Instead, she chose to talk of rainbows and shelves and parrots on the chandelier. Anything except Judge Todd Cunningham's cause.

"I love rainbows. Don't you? They're full of promise." She leaned down and picked up her broken shelf. "It looks like we'll have to start all over. Are you really good at carpentry?" She didn't wait for an answer. "We'll put the shelf over there. Of course, Hortense will probably think it's a perch built especially for her. That's what she thinks about the chandelier. Naughty bird. Are you sure you don't mind building a shelf on your day off? There must be dozens of other things you want to do . . . like sailing."

She ran out of breath, her cheeks quite pink from the effort of talking so much. Todd thought she had stopped at exactly the right time. "We'll go sailing after we build the shelf."

"No."

"Why not?"

"I can't think of a reason right now."

"Could it be the Chinese fortune?"

"What do you know about the Chinese fortune?"

"I have a friend at the Chinese restaurant where I bought the cookies. I had been planning on asking you to dinner anyhow." As he looked down at her rosy face, he could hardly resist the urge to touch her.

"But you don't know which fortune I got."

"One plus one equals happiness."

"How did you know that?"

"I think that fortune has a nice ring. Don't you?" He grinned. "I had my friend put it in all the cookies."

"Sneaky."

"How else could I know that you got the right one?"

"I don't believe in fortunes."

"Then why do your cheeks have roses?"

The temptation was too great, he thought. How could he stand here in Wonderland and not touch his enchanting Amy? He reached out both hands and smoothed her hair back from her flushed face. Her skin was velvety-smooth and slightly damp from the heat and her exertions. And it felt exactly right. It felt so right that he let his hand linger on her face.

Amy was glowing inside and out from his touch. She thought she might just stand there amid her clutter until she floated off on a cloud, or at least until Christmas. She had missed a man's touch. Not until that moment did she know how much.

Without thinking she covered his hands with hers. It was one of those spontaneous gestures that never would have happened if she had paused to consider her reasons.

"Your hands feel so good on my face," she said. "I wish they could stay there forever."

"We'll see about that, Amy," he said as he lowered his lips to hers.

The kiss lasted through another one of Hortense's tirades. It lasted through Aunt Syl's breakfast. It lasted until both Todd and Amy had forgotten what they had started out to do. It lasted until they both wished for a private bower instead of an apartment with a ready-made audience.

At last Todd lifted his head. "What was it we were going to do?"

"Move these boxes?"

"That's as good an idea as any."

They spent the rest of the morning moving boxes back to the closet. They were so enchanted with each other that they completely forgot they had intended to build shelves.

Todd looked at Amy over the boxes and wanted to take her into his arms.

She looked at him over the boxes and wanted to kiss him.

His arm brushed against hers. Deliberately.

She bumped into him. Not quite accidentally.

He opened his mouth to say *I'm falling in love*

with you, but remained silent. He was afraid of pushing her too fast, too soon.

She started to tell him how much she liked him, but she didn't. She was afraid of being vulnerable.

Once he dropped a box on his toe. His muttered "damn" was not because of the box but because of another missed opportunity. He wondered how much longer he could restrain himself. He wondered how many more times he could see Amy without taking her into his arms and making love to her. He thought that such restraint might give him a heart attack. He even thought of appealing his case to Amy to see if she would make love with him simply as a preventive measure.

More than once Amy forgot which way the closet was. It made her wonder.

When Todd finally left, he forgot his cup.

Seven

Amy's second day in court wasn't nearly as terrifying as her first. Todd winked at her as she scooted into her seat to await her turn before the judge's bench. He had bolstered her courage so much that she even winked back. As a matter of fact, she thought she might disturb the peace again just so she could come to court and see him in his robes. He looked dignified and imposing. Princely. Solid. Endurable. He looked like a man who could conquer anything, even death. She squelched the urge to run up to the bench and stroke her hands across his broad shoulders just to see if he was real.

She spent most of her day in court studying the judge. It seemed a safe enough thing to do, especially since he was sitting on a platform and she was way in the back of the courtroom, out of reach. She wondered why, as much as she loved touching, that touching Todd Cunningham disturbed her. Then she decided she wouldn't think about it. The ceiling fans were lazily stirring the humid air, and the day was much too hot for

introspection. She tried to force her attention away
from Todd, but he would no longer be denied. He
was at the front of the courtroom, solid and un-
avoidable. He was a tangible part of her present,
not some ephemeral dream of her past. Now that
she had put away the seascapes and the pipe,
wasn't it time to move forward? she asked herself. Wasn't it time to embrace the present and
live, really live?

She studied the face that had become dear to
her. She hadn't realized how dear until that moment. It wasn't just that he was handsome and
princely in his judicial robes. It wasn't simply the
stunning blue of his eyes and the thick cap of
dark hair that drew her to him. It was the man
himself. His humor and compassion, the way he
was strong when she need strength and lighthearted when she needed cheering up.

Here was a man who had come unbidden into
her life, a man who offered her more than friend-
ship, more than companionship. He offered her
passion and joy. Did she dare reach out for him?
Did she dare risk loving and losing again? She
didn't know. All she knew was that his charm was
fatal. With a certainty that comes from self-analysis,
Amy realized she could never again walk away
from his embrace.

She smiled. She could only guess when the time
would come, but when it did, she would not turn
away. She wouldn't ponder the future or the past.
She was going to live for the moment. Starting
now.

With that thought she turned her attention away
from Todd and onto her accuser, Mrs. Matilda
Hildenbrand. The matriarch of Baltimore society
glared down her long nose at Amy, scowling as if

she had just caught sight of an odious bug. The look put Amy on the defensive. Although she was sorry the picnic had been ruined, she wasn't sorry enough to roll over and play dead. She had come into the courtroom prepared to enter another guilty plea and have the business over with, but Mrs. Matilda Hildenbrand's look of contempt made her change her mind. She vowed that today she wouldn't be putty in anybody's hands. It was a day for momentous decisions, she thought as she slipped from her seat to call her aunt Syl.

"I need Herman," she said over the phone. "Can you bring him down?"

"Of course." Even over the phone Aunt Syl's voice vibrated with good cheer. "My curiosity is killing me. Why do you want Herman? I thought you and Todd had worked everything out."

"I've changed my mind about pleading guilty."

"Goody. Herman and I will be right there."

Amy waited in the hall until Aunt Syl and Herman arrived. Then the strange crew slipped into the back of the courtroom. When her name was finally called, Amy pressed Herman's switches and led him to the front. A murmur went through the room as the little robot whirred toward the judge's bench.

Todd hadn't missed a thing—Amy's exit from the courtroom, her return with the robot. He wondered what in the devil she was up to. Only years of habit enabled him to keep his face solemn as he looked down at her.

"Amy Logan, how do you wish to plead to charges of disturbing the peace?"

"Not guilty, your honor." Amy was proud of herself. Gone was the timidity that had marked her first day in court. She spoke so loudly that Mrs.

Matilda Hildenbrand nearly jumped out of her seat. Amy's plea was so forceful that even Todd was a bit rattled.

"Who is pleading your case?" he asked.

"I am."

He didn't bat an eyelash at the news. Now that the first shock of her bold move was over, he was eager to see what she would do next.

He heard the plaintiff's story first. It took all his willpower to sit patiently through Mrs. Hildenbrand's rambling account of a summer picnic gone awry. With dramatic gestures she painted such a villainous role for Amy that even the onlookers occasionally muttered in disbelief. There was a collective sigh of relief when the woman sat down and Amy approached the bench to speak in her defense.

She began her plea with simple eloquence.

"I plead not guilty, your honor, because I didn't disturb Mrs. Hildenbrand's summer picnic. A stray cat did."

Todd couldn't suppress his smile. He remembered how frightened Amy had been the last time she had been in his courtroom. He approved her newfound confidence.

Encouraged by his smile, she continued. "My robot . . ." She stopped and punched instructions into Herman's computer panel. "Say hello to the people, Herman." The little robot turned toward the packed courtroom and saluted. The crowd applauded. "As I was saying," Amy continued, "my robot and I were merely walking down the street, when a stray cat crossed our path. The cat became frightened and ran up a tree bordering Mrs. Hildenbrand's yard. The blue jays in the tree flew down into her yard and frightened the members of the Ladies' Auxiliary. Hearing the screaming, I climbed over the fence to see what I could do. If I had stayed on the other side of the fence, your honor, Mrs. Hildenbrand would have had to charge the cat and the blue jays with disturbing the peace because she wouldn't even have known I exist. My only crime is in being a good Samaritan. Should I have to pay for that crime? Should I be charged because a stray cat became frightened? Am I responsible for the behavior of all the cats in Baltimore?"

A loud "No!" resounded throughout the courtroom. Although Todd hated to reprimand Amy's Greek chorus of supporters, he banged his gavel.

"Order in the court," he demanded.

Mrs. Hildenbrand turned and stared at the crowd, apparently stunned to find public opinion so against her.

Someone from the back of the room called, "Looks like every cat in Baltimore will have to be brought to justice for disturbing the peace."

Everyone started laughing, and even Todd had to bend down on the pretext of examining his notes to hide his smile. For the life of him, he couldn't figure out what he had to smile about. Not only had Amy disrupted his quiet home, she had now turned his courtroom upside down. But through it all she had maintained an innocence and vulnerability that made him want to go out and slay dragons for her.

When he looked up again a moment later and pounded his gavel, calling for order, Mrs. Hildenbrand rose to her feet. As the courtroom refused to come to order, she opened and closed her mouth several times, unable to speak, then finally threw up her hands in exasperation.

"This is ridiculous!" she exclaimed. "I withdraw the charges!"

The spectators cheered. Amy's eyes widened, then she smiled with relief and happiness.

"Case dismissed," Todd declared, and banged his gavel down once. To be honest, he was relieved too.

As Mrs. Hildenbrand swept from the courtroom, Amy considered going home as well. Then she glanced at Todd, and when their eyes briefly met she decided to stay until he was through. She told Aunt Syl to take Herman home, then slipped into a seat in the back, prepared to wait patiently.

Justice had never been dispensed so quickly as Todd hurried through the rest of the cases on the docket. After the last case had been dispatched and the courtroom had emptied, he took Amy's arm and started leading her to his office.

"I must say I'm relieved Mrs. Hildenbrand withdrew the charges," he said.

"Why?" Amy asked. She felt like a cork bobbing along in the lee of a great ship as she followed Todd. Being attached to all that steadiness and solidity was a pleasant feeling.

He stopped at his office door and looked down at her. "Because as I listened to you defending yourself, I realized I couldn't judge you impartially. I realized . . ."

He stopped, pushed open the door, and ushered her inside his office. He locked the door, then with slow deliberation shed his judicial robe. Amy's heart tripped into double time as she watched him hang it in a closet. He strode back across the room to her, halting when he was only inches away.

"If Mrs. Hildenbrand hadn't dropped the charges,"

she asked, "what would you have ruled?" She meant the question to be light and teasing, but her voice was oddly husky.

"Amy Logan, if I could, I would sentence you to life."

"In prison?" Her question was purely rhetorical. She saw destiny shining in his eyes.

"In my arms."

They came together, seemingly in slow motion. Without hurry he put his arms around her slight shoulders and pulled her against his chest. The soft hair at her temple stirred as his lips sought the golden strands.

"You are my rainbow, Amy."

She hid her smile against his chest. "Why?"

"I don't know. Who can explain joy?" He tipped her face up with a finger. "Who can explain how one woman out of the dozens I've known has the ability to wrap herself around my heart? I'm falling in love with you, Amy Logan."

His lips descended on hers before she could protest. And then there was no more need for denial. The kiss said it all. Until Todd, she had never known that kisses were like this—erotic, unbridled, a pulsing imitation of lovemaking. Her arms slipped around his neck, and she wound her fingers in his crisp hair. As his tongue explored the warm depths of her mouth, she was more than compliant. She was eager—eager to know and to be known, eager to take that one final step that would catapult her over the barriers of the past.

Her nipples hardened against his chest, and she went limp in his arms as the drugging effect of the kiss swamped her. She welcomed the invasion of his tongue and answered its insistent thrusts with tiny moans of desire.

Only when she felt his hands move across the front of her blouse did she rouse herself enough to protest.

"Todd?" The small question in her voice made him pause.

"Don't fight it, Amy."

"Maybe we should talk."

"We've gone beyond talking. I love you. What more is there to say?"

"I can't say those words to you. Not yet."

"It doesn't matter. I want you."

"Here?"

"Here. Now."

"Todd . . ." Her voice trailed off in a breathless whisper. What more could she say? There was no need to deny that she wanted him. Her body had already betrayed her. She had known from the moment he had kissed her in the soap bubbles— perhaps even before—that they were destined to be together. What did it matter how or where or when? She could run from love until she dropped from exhaustion, but it would not be denied. "Todd," she said again, and it was a soft sigh of acquiescence.

He needed no more invitation. He unbuttoned her blouse and pushed aside the restraining material, slipping it down her arms. "You're beautiful," he breathed as he saw her small breasts, high and perfectly formed, pressing against the lacy restraints of her bra. With slow reverence he released them. Amy's head fell backward on a limp neck as his thumbs moved back and forth on her breasts, coaxing the nipples into hardened peaks of desire.

"How I've wanted this," he said as he lowered his lips to take the burgeoning crests into his mouth. His lips and tongue teased, tugged, caressed.

It was magic. New sensations exploded in Amy, leaving her trembling and gasping. Tim, her gentle artist husband, had rarely taken the time to engage in erotic foreplay. Theirs had always been a gentle, unimaginative coupling, almost sedate in its lack of fire and passion.

As Todd continued the sweet tugging, she went moist with need. A stifled moan escaped her lips, and he answered it by backing her across the room and lowering her to his sofa. She welcomed the leathery softness against her back.

His mouth moved upward to nuzzle her neck as his hands quickly divested her of skirt, half-slip, and panties. He dispatched his own clothes with the same sureness. Feeling his bold maleness press against her naked flesh, she tipped off the edge of the earth.

He captured her mouth once more as his hands explored her body. His fingers traced her curves, caressing, memorizing. He touched her surely, intimately. She arched against the probing fingers, spiraling upward on a never-ending curve of desire.

Their mouths melted together as he drew out the anticipation. His fingers coaxed; she responded. Her breath came in ragged spurts until she felt the shudder of her surrender.

She could have stayed in his arms forever, content to lie beneath him. She opened her eyes. Todd was gazing down at her with a mixture of awe and tenderness.

"My Amy," he whispered, bending down to kiss her neck.

She could feel the tension in his shoulders, sense his tight control.

"Now?" His voice was thick with unleashed passion.

"Yes," she breathed.

She felt him part her legs and slip inside. Their combined sighs sounded like the summer winds on the Chesapeake. They rocked together in gentle rhythm, slowly absorbing the wonder of their joining. Then the winds quickened until they became a gale. They rode the storm together, each searching motion of their bodies escalating the fierceness of the winds that shook them.

Todd waited, his control almost a palpable thing in the quietness of the chambers. Only after Amy cried out her release did he allow himself his own ecstatic completion. .

His sweat-dampened chest relaxed against hers, and she could feel the thunderous rhythm of his heart. She ran her hands lightly along his back, memorizing the feel of him. She wanted to hold this moment to herself forever.

"Amy?" His voice was muffled against her hair.

"Shh. Don't talk. I just want to absorb you."

Her hands made lazy circles on his back as her senses took in the setting. The leather under her felt soft and warm, slick with the sweat of their passion. Overhead the ceiling fan stirred the heavy air. Its almost useless whirring sounded loud in the quiet room. A noisy fly hummed near their heads, then moved on to light on a marble-top table. The burnished mahogany walls seemed to have absorbed the sunlight. Their polished red-gold surrounded her like a benediction. A stray sunbeam, drifting through the partly closed shutters, caught the swirling dust motes on the old hardwood floor.

The room exuded solidity and permanence. It closed them away from the real world of strivings and disappointments. It wrapped them in serenity. To Amy's heightened senses, the room spoke love.

She sighed against Todd's neck.

"Amy?" He lifted his head and looked down at her, searching her face for any sign of regret. All he saw was contentment. He planted a tender kiss on her forehead. "Come back with me."

"Where?"

"To my apartment."

"I'm not sure . . ."

"I am. I'm sure enough for both of us."

"Aunt Syl . . ."

". . . will approve."

Amy laughed. "You're right. She'll probably even applaud."

"Does that mean yes?"

"It means maybe."

"Then I'll have to convince you." He lowered his lips to her neck. The sensuous kisses made her shiver.

"Hmmm," she murmured.

"Is that a yes?"

"Not yet."

His mouth moved downward to take possession of one ripe nipple.

She gasped.

"Yes?" His voice was muffled against her satin flesh.

"Keep convincing me."

And he did.

By the time the convincing was over, the sun had dropped low in the western sky and the judge's chambers were shadowed with purple.

Todd's laugh was exultant as he sat up and pulled Amy into his arms. "This staid old courthouse has never known such excitement."

She playfully punched his cheek. "And you a judge. You ought to be ashamed of yourself."

"I am. Mortified." But he didn't look mortified at all. Amy thought he looked like a pleased little boy who had just outwitted a roomful of adults.

She snuggled against him, completely at ease in her nakedness. "Do you reprimand all criminals this way?"

"Only those who disturb the peace."

"Then I'll have to disturb the peace more often."

"How about twice a day?"

"Twice?"

"All right. You win. Three times a day."

"It might interfere with other things . . . like eating."

"That's okay. I can live on love." He released her and reached for his pants. "I hate to leave."

"Then let's stay." The suggestion just popped out. Amy knew that as long as they stayed in these chambers they were removed from the real world, set apart from all the bad things that could happen.

"We will if you don't mind an audience," Todd said.

"Who?"

"The night watchman."

"In that case . . ." She stood up and started dressing.

"We'll call your aunt from my place."

"I didn't say yes."

"You didn't say no."

She caught her lower lip between her teeth. What harm could there be? she wondered. After all, he wasn't proposing marriage. He wasn't asking for a longtime commitment. He was simply inviting her to his apartment for shared pleasure.

She took his hand. "I'll come."

He squeezed her hand. "Remind me to send Mrs. Matilda Hildenbrand a dozen red roses."

Todd had been right; Aunt Syl was delighted when Amy called her.

"I'm going to New York for the weekend, anyway," she told her niece. "Now I won't worry about you being alone."

"You never mentioned a trip to New York."

"Didn't I? It must have slipped my mind." Aunt Syl's feigned innocence didn't fool Amy. "I'm even taking Hortense, so you won't have to worry about a thing. Just concentrate on the judge."

Amy laughed. "I'll have to ask his permission first." Covering the receiver with her hand, she turned and asked Todd, "Is it all right if I concentrate on you this weekend?"

For an answer he put his arms around her from behind and pulled her roughly against his chest. "If you concentrate on anything else, I'll have you back in court so fast your head will spin."

"In the judge's chambers?" Forgetting about the receiver dangling in her hand, she turned and put her arms around his neck.

"Where else?" The kiss he gave her might have gone on forever if the squawking of the telephone hadn't finally caught their attention.

Amy was flushed and breathless when she pulled

away. "I forgot Aunt Syl." She pulled the receiver up by the cord. "Aunt Syl?"

"I'm still here, dear, although I must say the heat coming from that end has nearly melted the phone. Why don't you hang up, Amy, and get on with the romance?"

" 'Bye. Enjoy New York."

"More to the point, dear, New York will enjoy me."

Todd untangled them from the cord and hung up the phone.

"Now," he said, "where were we?"

Amy unfastened the first button of his shirt and kissed him on the chest. "Here," she said.

He slid his open mouth down her cheek. "I thought it was here." His questing mouth moved over her throat. "Or here." She tipped her head back, and he pushed her blouse aside and captured a breast. "Or here."

There was no more time for words. He scooped her into his arms and carried her to his bedroom. She had a fleeting impression of heavy furniture and ordered masculinity before she was once more lost in the magic of his embrace.

By the time the magic ended, the first pale fingers of a summer moon lay across the bedcovers.

"One of us should be thinking about food," Todd said.

Amy stretched drowsily and snuggled closer to him. "I thought you said you could live on love."

"I lied."

"Is that a habit of yours?"

"Yes. It came in handy when I was a child. Got me out of all sorts of scrapes."

"I wish I had had brothers and sisters."

"I wish you had, too, love. Having a family is like having a safe port in a storm."

"Of course, I had Aunt Syl. And Hortense."

His arm tightened around her shoulders. "And now you have me."

And now you have me. The words seemed to echo in her mind. Did she really have him? she wondered. He felt solid and lasting, but how did she know . . . She wouldn't even let herself finish the thought. Almost desperately she turned her face into his chest. Her mouth blazed a hot trail of nibbling kisses through the dark crisp mat of hair.

She absolutely refused to think any further than this weekend. She put on a brave smile and raised her head to look at him. "Do you intend to keep me captive in this bedroom, or do you intend to feed me?"

"That's not a bad idea."

"The food?"

"No. The captive part."

"I'm in lo—" She stopped to correct herself. "—bed with a tyrant." Dragging the sheet with her, she bounced to the floor. With expert motions she fashioned a sarong. "That will have to do since all my worldly belongings are upstairs."

His broad smile showed his admiration of her attire. "I like that. How did you learn that trick?"

"It's no trick; it's an art. I spent some time in India with Aunt Syl."

He reached over and traced one bare shoulder. "What would happen if I untied the knot?"

"Don't you dare. Unless you want me to cook in the nude."

"That's a wonderful idea." His fingers inched closer to the knot.

She playfully swatted his hand away. "What if grease splattered on me?"

"I would apply burn remedy."

He hopped out of bed and stood before her, splendid in his nakedness. Her knees went weak at the sight of him, and her nipples tightened into erotic rosebuds. She had never known that merely seeing a man could arouse such feelings. Todd had awakened a sexuality she hadn't known she possessed.

He stood in the moonlight, smiling at her, then suddenly reached over and untied the knot. The bed sheet slithered to the floor.

"I vote for a bath before we eat," he said.

She stood very still, loving the way his gaze blazed over her body. "Is this a democracy?"

"No. It's a dictatorship." He lifted her into his arms and carried her into the bathroom.

Eight

Todd's tub was enormous, more than big enough to accommodate two feisty lovers. They cavorted in the bubbles like naughty children.

"I've never kissed a man with a bubble beard," Amy said. "I like it."

"Then I'll grow one."

"A bubble beard?"

"Certainly. I'll do anything for my China doll."

"Anything?"

"That's what I said."

"Then pass the soap. You're hogging it."

"You're easy to please. You could have kingdoms laid at your feet, and you ask for soap."

"You haven't heard the rest. I want you to scrub my back."

"Here?"

"Yes. There . . . and there . . . And oh, yes, there."

"What about here?"

"Todd! That's not my back."

"Didn't I tell you? I don't know back from front."

"A convenient disability."

"Handy."

"Wonderful."

"Downright sinful."

"Positively . . . hmmmm, Todd."

They stayed in the tub until Amy declared she had shriveled to a prune. Todd said wickedly that he ate prunes for breakfast. She told him that it would soon be breakfast and not dinner if they didn't quit horsing around. He said he never knew horses had so much fun. She swatted him with a towel.

Amy dressed in Todd's shirt and he wore jeans. In the kitchen, dinner preparation became a bawdy romp.

"Stir this, Amy."

"But that's steak."

"I know. Stir it anyway."

"Why?"

"Because you jiggle when you stir."

"How do you know?"

"You jiggled the night we cooked Chinese food."

"You rascal. You weren't cooking; you were watching me."

"Guilty."

"Is that why you were squeezing the egg rolls?"

"Just be quiet and stir the steak, Amy."

After dinner Todd told Amy he was going to give her an introduction to his bed. She said she had already been properly introduced. He said he wanted to give her an improper introduction.

He did.

"Wake up, Amy."

She pried one eye open. "I just got to sleep," she said.

"Hurry or we'll miss the sunrise." Todd pulled her out of bed and stood her on her feet. He laughed when she threatened to topple. "Upsy daisy, sailor," he said as he steadied her. "You'll have your sea legs in a minute."

She peered groggily around. "Sea? I thought this was your bedroom."

"It is. But in a jiffy we'll be on the boat. Run upstairs and get your swimsuit."

"Run?" She yawned. "I can barely stand. Is this a sane weekend affair or a survival contest?"

"Neither. It's love." He picked up her purse and rummaged in it for her keys. "Tell me where you keep your swimsuit."

"In my bedroom." She sank onto the bed. "Closet." She lay down. "Top shelf." She pulled the covers over her head.

"I'll be back in a jiffy."

"Don't hurry on my account." She was asleep again before he got to the front door.

Amy marveled that she was actually wide awake on Todd's boat watching the sunrise.

"It's gorgeous," she said. "I wouldn't have missed it for anything in the world."

"That's not what you told me half an hour ago."

"What did I tell you?"

"You said you would kill for another hour of sleep."

"I didn't know what I would be missing."

She turned her face to the east and watched the flamboyant sun preen itself in the mirror of the Chesapeake. Brilliant pools of red spilled across the waters. Gold, so bright it almost hurt the eyes, gilded the waves and burnished the sails.

Without realizing it, Amy was a part of the morning beauty. Todd stood transfixed as the sun made her skin glow. With her fair hair and blue swimsuit, she seemed to be one with the sun and the sea. A sense of well-being washed over his soul, and he knew he was experiencing a moment that would be forever engraved in his memory.

After the colors had faded from the water and the sun had risen above the horizon, Amy turned back to Todd.

"Thank you," she said simply. "I'll always treasure this moment."

"The best is yet to come." He moved swiftly across the deck and took her in his arms. "After the sunrise comes the loving." He lowered her to a blanket.

She shuddered as the familiar heat started in her loins and spread throughout her body. "What about other boats?" she asked, but her protest was mild. At Todd nudged her swimsuit straps aside with his mouth, she didn't care if the whole world witnessed their union. She was that happy.

"This cove is secluded," he murmured. "It was designed especially for us." He peeled away the rest of her skimpy suit and tossed it onto the deck.

Only nature witnessed what happened next.

Afterward Todd sailed into shallow waters and moored the sloop. Taking nets, they climbed over the side and trapped enough crabs for breakfast. Todd built a fire on the beach, and they carried on in the tradition of newfound lovers while their food steamed.

"I hope this day never ends," Amy said while they were enjoying their morning's catch.

"It doesn't have to. Marry me, Amy."

She ate three more bites of crab before answering. "I can't."

"Give me one good reason why not."

"Be—"

"If you say 'because,' I'm going to leave you stranded in this cove."

She laughed. "I love you, Todd."

"Say that again."

"I love you."

"That's all the answer I need. We'll have a big family wedding. You'll love my brothers. In fact, you'll meet them next Tuesday. I'm having a small party—"

"I didn't say yes."

"To the proposal or to the party?"

"Both."

"You said you loved me."

"It's not the same thing."

"Yes, it is."

She pushed aside her paper plate of steamed crab and stood up. "This is all happening too fast, Todd. I need more time."

He was silent as she paced the beach. "I hadn't even meant to say 'I love you.' It just popped out. I guess I wasn't fully aware of it myself until this very moment." She stopped pacing and dug her toes into the sand, staring down at the small indentations she was making. "I can't say yes right now, Todd. Please don't push me."

He stood swiftly and pulled her into his arms. Without saying a word he rocked her gently. His lips caressed her hair as he silently communicated his understanding.

The sail back to their apartment was subdued.

They sat side by side in the boat, their hands clasped in mutual need.

Amy suggested they spend the rest of the weekend in her apartment.

"Who knows," she said half in jest, "after seeing what a disorganized woman I am, you might change your mind about wanting to marry me."

"Never," he said as he followed her inside. He stubbed his toe on a hammer when he said it.

"See what I mean?"

He bent over and rubbed his toe. "My oldest brother, Jeff, is always telling me I need more adventure in my life."

"You've come to the right place. If you're lucky, Aunt Syl might even hang you out the window."

"I can hardly wait." He carefully made his way between the toolbox and the birdcage. The lone seascape on the wall had caught his attention.

Amy watched him studying the painting. She loved the way he stood, his body relaxed, his expression serene. He seemed to have infinite patience. She wondered if she had made a mistake in saying no to him. She loved him. There was no denying that. How long she had loved him she couldn't be sure. Perhaps she had loved him from the moment she had seen him standing beneath her window. Perhaps the love had been growing all along without her awareness. She thought that sometimes love was like that—a subtle flourishing rather than a sudden attack.

She gazed at the painting. Tim's painting. A few short days ago when she had put away his paintings, she had never dreamed she would be saying she loved another man. She was glad her healing was complete.

"How did he die?" Todd asked the question without turning around.

"He drowned." Saying the words aloud was almost a catharsis for Amy. She crossed the room and stood beside Todd, looking up at the painting. "Ironic, isn't it, that the one thing he loved most in the world finally claimed his life."

Todd reached out and squeezed her hand.

"He was always painting water," she continued. "He used to say it had many moods and he wanted to capture them all. The sea was almost his obsession." Now that she had released the words, they flowed out. The more she talked about her husband's death, the better she felt.

"He could sit for hours, sometimes never lifting his brush, simply gazing across the water. Now that I remember those times, I think I was a little jealous. I guess I never fully understood Tim."

"Does anyone ever fully understand another person?" Todd asked quietly. "Man is a complex creature, seen through a glass darkly."

She turned an appreciative look in his direction. "Sometimes you surprise me. You have the soul of a poet."

"Borrowed phrases."

"When you say them in that magnificent voice, you make them your own."

He pulled her into his arms. "Does that mean the woman loves me?"

She gave him a dazzling smile. "Why don't you find out?"

"Why, madame, you shock me, stuffy old judge that I am. It's high noon."

"What better time for love?"

She took his hand and led him into her bedroom. She flipped a switch on the headboard of her bed and the soft strains of "I'm in the Mood for Love" filled the room.

"Can I trust this bed?" Todd asked. The question was purely rhetorical. As he watched, Amy shucked her T-shirt and swimsuit and hopped into the middle of the bed. She looked so glorious sitting there naked, sun-polished and golden, that he wouldn't have cared if the bed had disturbed the entire town of Baltimore.

She stretched wantonly in the sunlight pouring through the window and smiled up at him archly. "The bed is trustworthy. I'm the one you should be worried about."

"That sounds ominous." His own T-shirt and swimming trunks fell in a heap on the floor. He stood beside the bed looking down at the woman he loved.

"Be forewarned," she said, stretching her hand out to him. He captured it and placed a lingering kiss in her palm. Anticipation built in her until she was breathless. "You asked me once to give you a warning."

He placed one knee on the mattress and knelt over her. "Do you plan to throw a window box in my direction?"

Amy thought she would drown in the blue of his eyes. "No." The word was barely a sigh. "I have other things in mind for you."

Without haste he lay down beside her, pressing his muscular length against her soft curves. "Why don't you show me?"

Her hair made a bright fan across his chest as she lifted her head to look down at him. She trailed her fingers along his chest. "This could take some time," she murmured. The fingers moved into the dark V of hair below his waist.

She felt him suck in his breath as her hand captured his pulsing manhood. "Maybe the rest of the day," she whispered as she lowered her head and covered him with her mouth.

"How about the rest of my life?"

Amy heard him but she didn't reply. She was lost in the wonder of love.

Todd's heart thudded against his ribs as her tongue teased him. Her hair, which had fallen across his thighs, felt like silk. Sensations built in him until he was writhing under her touch.

When he thought he would tip off the edge of the earth, he lifted her astride him. Theirs was a glorious joining, a summer jubilation. They arched together in the wash of sunlight.

And while they loved, the bed played on. The music mingled with their murmured words. It built and swelled around the heedless lovers. As the bed rocked and swayed, the music changed tempo. "I'm in the Mood for Love" sputtered to a halt and was replaced by a raucous blaring of trumpets.

The lovers didn't notice. They had their own brass band going. Their song lasted until they both shuddered to a climax. Amy stretched out limp across Todd's chest.

"Do you hear music?" he asked dreamily.

"Could be. Every time I'm near you, I hear music."

"Sounds like trumpets," he murmured as he brushed her damp hair off her temple.

"Hmmm. Angel trumpets." She flicked her tongue lazily across his mouth.

"The best kind." His hands bracketed her face. "I love you, Amy Logan."

"And I love you, Judge Todd Cunningham." She leaned down and pressed her mouth to his.

"Do you hear a loud banging?" he said against her lips.

"I think it's my heart."

"I think it's the door."

"Keep kissing and ignore it. I'm not expecting company."

"Amy."

"Hmmm?"

"I hear the door and trumpets." Suddenly he stiffened. "It's this damned bed again."

Amy sat bolt upright. "My Lord, the bed's playing 'Dixie.' " She started giggling. "Stand up and salute, Todd."

"I already did that."

She swatted him on the rump. "You call that saluting?"

He grinned wickedly. "What would you call it?"

"Heavenly."

He laughed and rolled out of bed. "One of us has to answer the door."

"It'll probably be a firing squad this time. You go."

Todd pulled on his damp, wrinkled swimsuit. "I never have my judicial robe when I need it." He raked a hand through his tousled hair. "How do I look?"

"Like you've spent the afternoon in bed." She flicked off the music. "What will you tell them?"

"That I've spent the afternoon in bed." He headed for the door.

"Todd!" she called, but he had already disappeared.

Amy sat in the middle of the tumbled covers and waited. Though she cocked her head toward the door, she couldn't hear a thing. She chuckled. Todd *did* look like he had spent the afternoon in bed, she thought. What would he tell the neighbors? If she hadn't been stark naked, she would have strolled through the sitting room to eavesdrop.

The minutes ticked by. A mosquito landed on Amy's leg and began to feast. She was so consumed by curiosity, she didn't even swat the pesky insect away. Perspiration trickled unnoticed down the side of her face as she waited for Todd's return.

When her curiosity had reached the explosion point, he strolled back into the bedroom.

"I'm dying to know what you told the neighbors," she said.

"Oh, this and that."

She thought his smile was perfectly outrageous. "Todd! Tell me."

"I'll tell you this much: the neighbors will never complain about this bed again. As a matter of fact, they're liable to stand up and salute the next time it plays 'Dixie.' "

Amy turned bright pink all over. "You didn't tell them . . ."

"Last one in the shower has to scrub my back." He disappeared into the bathroom and was already under the water, humming, by the time Amy arrived.

"Scrub your back, indeed," she grumbled as she squeezed into the tiny stall beside him. "That wasn't even a fair challenge."

"Use lots of soap, Amy. I'm partial to soap."

She washed his back with unnecessary vigor. "Did you say we were . . ."

"You missed a spot."

"You didn't mention . . ."

"A little to the left."

She threw the washcloth at his back. "You're mean. Scrub your own back."

He turned around and squeezed her to his chest. "Do you know what happened to the cat, Amy?"

"The one that put me in the courtroom?"

"No. Just any old cat."

As the soapy-slick feeling of his body against hers invaded her senses, her curiosity was replaced by desire. She peppered leisurely kisses across his chest before she answered him.

"What happened to the cat, Todd?"

"You're making me forget."

Her tongue made teasing motions around his nipple. "Finish the story. You know how I love your stories."

"Curiosity"—he bent and flicked his tongue in her ear—"killed"—he stooped to nuzzle her neck—"the cat." He captured her lips.

She pulled away. "How did it die?"

"Now who's being mean?" He pulled her roughly back to him. "I'll show you."

And he did.

A small eternity later he let her slide back down his body until her feet touched the shower floor.

"Lucky cat," she sighed.

They called Aunt Syl that evening.

"She always stays at the Waldorf," Amy told Todd as she dialed the number.

The phone rang three times with no answer. She began to feel anxious.

"Answer," she pleaded. Her eyes were enormous as she looked up at Todd. "She was tired the other evening when she came home from the concert."

"I'm here." He put his hands on her shoulders and massaged the back of her neck. "Don't borrow trouble, love."

Aunt Syl answered on the sixth ring. Amy went limp with relief.

"Aunt Syl! Where on earth have you been?"

"To Saks and Bloomingdale's and Macy's. You should have seen the dinner I had at Tavern-on-the-Green. I've been to Broadway and Central Park. I ate hot dogs and listened to a street concert. You sound breathless, dear. What's the matter with you?"

"Nothing." Amy looked up at Todd and smiled. "It's so good to hear your voice. How are you?"

"The same as I was day before yesterday: chipper as a grasshopper and twice as feisty as most women my age. Is Todd there with you?"

"Yes."

"Then why are you wasting your time talking to me? Can't you two think of something more exciting to do?"

"We already have."

Aunt Syl's laugh was so hearty, even Todd heard it. "Well, if you've run out of ideas, turn to page 88 in my last book. That ought to keep you busy for a while."

"You're a naughty old woman."

"I know. But at least I'm not dull. 'Bye, Amy."

"Take care, Aunt Syl." Smiling, Amy cradled the receiver. "She's all right," she told Todd.

"From what I gathered, she's more than all right. Your Aunt Syl is a remarkable woman, Amy."

"I wish she could live forever."

Todd looked into the face of the woman who had loved and lost so often. First her parents and then her husband. He wanted to protect her from sorrow, shield her from loss, but he knew he couldn't. Life dealt bad cards along with the good, he thought. The best anyone could do was try to stay in the game.

He put his arm around her shoulders and squeezed.

"Do you know what I wish?" he asked.

"What?"

"I wish I had a double fudge sundae with three scoops of whipped cream. How do you feel about a quick visit to Swenson's?"

Amy beamed. "At last! I thought you would never get around to food."

"Can I help it if the lady distracts me?"

The moon made dappled shadows across the musical bed. Amy slept with one arm on Todd's chest and her head cradled on his shoulder. She tossed fitfully, her sleep disturbed by a dream. It was the same dream she had had since childhood. The characters changed but the setting was always the same. She was standing in a thick fog, reaching out for people who were no longer there. After her parents' death she had reached through the fog for them. Tim had been the elusive dream character after his death.

Tonight the dream was particularly disturbing. Todd was the one who stood out of reach in the fog. She ran toward him, her hands outstretched, and found herself clutching emptiness. He would reappear, and once more she would reach for him. Thick fog would separate them again.

"No," she moaned in her sleep.

Todd was instantly awake. "Amy?" He raised

himself on an elbow and looked down at her sleeping face. He saw the agony there.

"No. Todd. No." She tossed restlessly.

He cradled her close and stroked her face. "I'm here, love. I'm here."

"Todd?" She opened her eyes. "You're here." She clung to him. "Thank heavens, you're all right."

He brushed her hair back from her forehead. "Of course I'm all right. You just had a bad dream, love."

"You were there in the fog and I couldn't find you. You kept disappearing . . . like my parents . . . like Tim." Her nails dug into his back.

"Do you want to talk about it, Amy?"

"Just hold me, Todd. Hold me."

He held her, caressing her gently, until she fell asleep. But he stayed awake a long time pondering the significance of her dream.

Amy was subdued the next morning. Todd noticed her quietness. As they prepared breakfast he wondered at the way she seemed to ease around him, avoiding touching.

"Is anything wrong, Amy?" he asked.

"It's Sunday. You'll be leaving today."

He laughed. "I'll only be going downstairs." He crossed the kitchen and put his hands on her shoulders. "And if I have my way, you'll be coming with me."

"No."

"Why live in separate apartments when we love each other? Besides, we need to be together so we can plan a big family wedding."

"No."

"If you keep saying that, I'm going to develop a complex."

"I won't be moving in with you, Todd."

Her face was set and white. He felt a small prickle of fear. His attempted laugh was hollow.

"All right. Since you're such an old-fashioned woman, you can wait until after the wedding before moving in."

She lifted her hand as if warding off disaster. "Please don't talk about weddings, Todd. I never said yes." She shrugged out of his grasp and turned her back to him.

The small prickle of fear became full-fledged alarm. "Okay. I'm being pushy. I admit it. It's just that I see no point in waiting when we love each other."

She made no reply.

"You do love me, don't you, Amy?" he asked quietly.

Clenching her fists behind her back, she turned to face him. "We've had a lovely weekend affair. Let it go at that."

"I won't accept that. What we've had is more than a weekend affair."

"You have to accept it. I was wrong about—" She stopped and bit her lower lip. Telling this lie was going to be the hardest thing she ever had to do.

"Go on." His voice had an edge of steel in it.

"I was wrong about loving you. I made a mistake."

"You could have fooled me."

She turned her hands palms-up in an eloquent attempt at nonchalance. "So . . . I enjoy loving. My body sometimes says things my heart doesn't mean."

"Say the words, Amy."

"What words?"

"Say, 'Todd, I don't love you.' "

"Todd, I . . ." Her resolve faltered as she looked at his face. How could she deny love when her whole being ached with the need of him?

"You can't say it." He crossed the small space that separated them and pulled her roughly against his chest. "Let's talk this out, Amy."

"No. Just go, Todd. I don't . . ."

"Say it," he said grimly, "and I'll go." He bent swiftly and captured her lips. It was an urgent kiss, a harsh kiss that brooked no denial.

Caught off guard, Amy responded instantly. Her mouth flowered open for the insistent thrusting of his tongue. As he roughly plunged into the honeyed depths of her mouth, she almost changed her mind. How could she let this man go? she wondered. How could she deny that she loved him when he had become her whole world? It took every ounce of her willpower to push herself out of his arms.

"Please go." Her voice shook as she said the words.

Seeing how distraught she was, Todd mentally kicked himself. Idiot, he raged inwardly. What she needed was understanding, not high-handed treatment.

"I'm sorry, Amy. I won't touch you again. Let's just sit down and discuss this over a cup of hot tea. We're two sane adults. There's no problem between us that can't be resolved."

"It's not between us. It's me. I can't handle this relationship."

"What we had is too good to be shrugged off so lightly."

"It was good while it lasted, Todd, but it's over. Finished."

"I'll go, Amy. I'll give you time—"

"I don't need time. My decision is final. I'll never change my mind."

"Never say never." He turned and stalked out of the apartment.

Amy stared at the closed door. She thought she might never feel joy again as long as she lived.

Nine

On Monday morning Aunt Syl and the petunias arrived at the same time.

Amy looked up from her invention. She managed a small smile for her aunt, but she wanted to scream when she saw Todd's butler holding the window box. Petunias spilled over the sides of the box in a riot of color. It was the rainbow Todd had promised her. Her face went white as she remembered those tender moments in the judge's chambers. Fortunately for her, nobody noticed. Aunt Syl and Justin were engaged in a lively discussion about petunias and concealed weapons

As she listened, Amy decided she would have enjoyed the conversation if her heart weren't broken in two.

"I could use a box of petunias in chapter nine," Aunt Syl said to Justin. "Nobody would notice a bloody knife in all those red blooms."

"A unique idea," Justin agreed. "Rather like Poe's 'Purloined Letter.' "

"Exactly!" Aunt Syl's dark eyes glittered with excitement as she tried to see beneath her tilted blond wig. She raked the wig back from her eyes, sending it farther askew. "Where do you want Justin to put this flower box, Amy?"

"I . . ." Amy caught her lower lip between her teeth. She didn't want the flowers. Seeing them would be a constant reminder of Todd. "I've changed my mind. Justin, please take them back to Judge Cunningham and tell him that I've changed my mind."

Aunt Syl looked at her niece, astonished. For the first time since she had entered the room, she noticed Amy's set face. Trouble was brewing in paradise, Aunt Syl decided, and incorrigible match-maker that she was, she was going to head it off at the pass.

"Nonsense," she said. "Why waste perfectly good petunias? Put the box at that window, Justin, and thank the judge kindly."

Justin smiled his gratitude at Aunt Syl as he carried the box to the window.

Amy didn't want to make a scene. Let him put the window box there, she thought. She'd simply not look at the flowers. She'd turn her head away every time she had to pass by. But not right now. Now she watched as Justin attached the box. Each hammer blow vibrated in her heart. How could she live without Todd? Whose broad shoulders would she cry on? Whose arms would she turn to? Where would she find joy?

After he finished attaching the box, Justin handed Amy a note. "From the judge," he said.

"Thank you, Justin." Amy stuck the note into her skirt pocket. She felt awkward and foolish with her stiff upper lip and her formality. She wanted to rush to the window box and bury her face in the rainbow of flowers. She wanted to laugh and cry at the same time. Instead, she gazed silently past the butler's beard until Aunt Syl rescued her.

Taking Justin's arm, Aunt Syl propelled him toward the door. "How lovely of you to bring the flowers! Let's have tea this afternoon and discuss knives. Maybe even hatchets. That Clyde gets worse every day." She laughed. "A real cad. Good-bye. Tell that perfectly wonderful judge Aunt Syl sends her regards."

She closed the door firmly behind Justin and turned back to her niece. "Now, tell me what's going on."

"Nothing. I had a weekend fling and it's over."

"*A fling!*" Aunt Syl's tone told Amy what she thought of that hateful word. "My dear, you've never had a fling in your life. One doesn't have flings with perfectly gorgeous men like the judge. One has a romantic interlude." She put her arm around Amy's shoulder, and her voice softened. "What's wrong? You look like you've lost your best friend."

"Maybe I have." Amy turned and buried her face in her aunt's bony shoulder. "I just couldn't handle it, that's all. Todd is wonderful, but I had to let him go."

Aunt Syl patted her head. "This will work itself out, dear." She looked at the flowers and smiled. "I'm sure of it. In the meantime, why don't we spend a perfectly frivolous afternoon exploring the city?"

Amy raised her head. "Are you sure you feel like it? Aren't you tired after your trip?"

"I feel positively rejuvenated. New York does that to me. Besides, I want to shock Baltimore with the new wig I bought. Wait till you see it. It's silver with streaks of hot pink."

They caught a trolley car into downtown Baltimore. Amy forgot about the note in her pocket as she and her aunt explored the city, laughing together like two teenagers. She was even able to forget Todd for a while.

But that evening her memories swamped her. Aunt Syl had gone to bed early, and Amy was trying to concentrate on a book. Todd's face kept superimposing itself over the words. His laughter echoed through the apartment. And the unopened note in her pocket grew heavier and heavier until it was a stone that had to be removed.

The paper rattled as she unfolded it. Todd's handwriting leaped out at her, bold and uncluttered. "You are still my rainbow," the note said.

Amy ran her fingers across the words, trying to capture the man through his writing. Her hands tingled, and her longing for Todd became a vast ache in the middle of her chest. For the first time since she had sent him away, she wondered if she had done the right thing. She wasn't even certain why she had ended the relationship. She knew only that it was better to lose him now, when the hurt would be small, than later, when the hurt would be a gaping hole that couldn't be filled.

She shoved the note back into her pocket and paced the floor. She had to get out of the apartment. She had to do something, anything, to relieve herself of the painful remembering.

Hastily she scribbled a note in case Aunt Syl should wake and find her gone. She ran a brush through her hair and hurried out the door.

She walked aimlessly at first, and then, after the theater marquee caught her eye, with purpose. She loved movies. If anything in the world could take her mind off her lost love, it would be a good movie. She bought her ticket without even bothering to see what was playing.

When she entered the theater lobby and smelled the popcorn, she knew she had made the right decision. A movie and popcorn, a double panacea. She bought a huge box of the buttered treat and slipped into a seat at the back of the darkened theater. She had the back row all to herself.

The first thing she noticed was the actor's blue eyes. Oh, Lord, she moaned to herself. Why did he have to have blue eyes? She stuffed popcorn into her mouth and tried not to think of Judge Todd Cunningham's remarkable blue eyes. Eyes that crinkled at the corners when he laughed, eyes that sparkled like the sun on the Chesapeake when he smiled, eyes that turned dark navy when he made love. She didn't hear a word the actor said. His hair was dark, too, almost as black as Todd's. She wondered if it felt crisp, like Todd's. She wondered if it would curl around her finger as if it had a mind of its own. She thought the actor shot somebody, but she wasn't sure.

Another late-night movie patron sat down beside her. She felt the hair rise on her arms as a leg brushed against hers, a muscular leg, a man's leg. She kept her eyes on the screen, wondering why he didn't sit somewhere else.

Suddenly she saw a big hand reach into her bucket of popcorn.

"Do you mind?" the man asked. "I forgot to buy some."

She jerked her head around at the sound of that familiar voice. Todd's smile lit up the theater.

"Are you following me?" she whispered fiercely.

"No. Are you following me?" He helped himself to her popcorn, deliberately resting one hand on her leg.

"I was here first."

"No, you weren't. I was sitting across the aisle and saw you come in."

The heat of his hand was beginning to make her lose her breath. She jerked her leg away, sending a spray of popcorn into the air.

"Careful," Todd said. "You're losing the popcorn."

"I'm also losing my temper. Go away!"

A round-faced woman sitting in front of them turned around. "Shhh!" she said.

Todd leaned over and whispered into Amy's ear. "Who do you think did it, love?"

She melted. And that irritated her even more. She had come to the movie to forget Todd, not to be invaded by him. "Did what?" she snapped.

The fat woman turned around again. "Shhh!"

"Sorry," Todd said. He leaned over and put his hand on Amy's leg again, making no pretense of getting popcorn. "The crime," he whispered. He was as close as he could get to her lips without actually touching them.

Amy thought she might die. She wanted to bop him with the popcorn box. She wanted to kiss him until his eyes crossed. She didn't really know what she wanted. Her words were a gentle sigh against his cheek. "What crime?"

His eyes sparkled in the dim light of the theater. "Haven't you been watching the movie, love?"

"How can I? Your head is in the way."

He settled back in his seat and swiftly pulled her head onto his shoulder. "There. Is that better?"

"No!" She quickly pulled away from him, "Why are you doing this?" she whispered.

When he turned toward her, his face was serious. "I have no intention of letting you go. I love you."

"And I have no intention of getting involved." She resolutely turned her face toward the screen. The actor with the blue eyes mocked her.

"You already are." With those cryptic words Todd, too, faced the screen.

The woman in front of them, having followed their conversation from start to finish, decided that the show behind her was more interesting than the one on the screen. She turned to face them. "It seems to me you two need to be working this out in bed instead of at the movies. Why don't you go home?"

"A brilliant suggestion," Todd said. He turned to Amy. "How about it, love? Shall we work this out in bed?"

"You're outrageous."

"You're adorable."

The woman in front of them beamed. "I love a good romance."

"This is not a romance," Amy told her. "It's going to be murder."

Todd put his arm around her shoulders. "It's going to be a wedding."

"Good." The woman smiled. "I love happy endings."

Amy decided to ignore them both. If she tried hard enough, she might even be able to pretend that Todd's arm wasn't sending a heated message to her body. She delved into the popcorn and turned her undivided attention to the screen. The dialogue made no sense to her and the action was meaningless, but she didn't care. She had to get her mind off the disturbing man at her side.

She sneaked a peek to see what he was doing. He caught her glance and winked. Turning away quickly, she feigned an interest in her popcorn. He reached into the box, capturing her hand in a slick, buttery grip. With slow deliberation he lifted her hand and licked each delicious fingertip.

"Ummm. Good," he said wickedly.

She should have pulled her hand away, but she didn't have the strength. Every inch of her had turned to maple syrup.

"Why don't you watch the movie?" she asked.

"I'd rather watch you." He savored another of her buttery fingers. "I'd rather eat you."

She tried to shut him out by closing her eyes. It didn't work. He was inside her head, inside her heart. Letting him go was going to be harder than she had ever imagined. Much harder.

He leaned over, his hot breath fanning her cheek. "I love you when you squinch your eyes shut like that." His lips seared her face from temple to jawline. "You can't shut me out that easily, Amy. Every time you open your eyes, I'll be there."

She opened her eyes and looked at him. "Like the Force?" They both smiled as they remembered the last time she had used those words.

"Exactly." Once more he pulled her head onto his shoulder. "Talk to me, Amy. Let me be your friend as well as your lover."

It would be so easy to talk to him, she thought, to dump all her problems on his broad shoulders. But she couldn't do that. She couldn't separate friend from lover. They were one and the same. And in order to survive, she had to cut herself off from both.

She stayed in the curve of his arm a moment

longer, absorbing the steady beat of his heart, soaking up his strength. At last, she pulled away.

"I'm going home," she said.

"I'm going with you."

"Todd . . ."

"I insist."

They left the dark theater. Outside, the garish marquee lights bathed them in green and red and purple.

"I don't know why you persist in this madness," Amy said as they walked down the street. "I'm not going to change my mind about you."

"Good."

"Good?"

"Yes. You've already told me that you love me."

"Not under oath."

He grinned. "You said it to a judge. That's the same thing."

She let that remark slide, thinking that silence would deter him. She was wrong.

"My party is tomorrow night. Be sure to bring Aunt Syl."

"I'm not coming."

"You must. You wouldn't want to disappoint my brothers, would you? They're expecting to meet the woman I love."

"Then you have approximately twenty-four hours to find another woman."

Their apartment building came into view. Amy's sigh of relief was audible.

"Your stubbornness is exceeded only by your beauty," Todd said as he opened the heavy door. Inside the foyer he pulled her into his arms. "Just so you have something to remember me by . . ."

His lips covered hers hungrily, and she could no more have walked away from his kiss than she could have sprouted wings and flown. She met the rapier thrusts of his tongue with soft cries of desire. In the semi-darkness of the hallway she almost gave up the past and became his. Almost, but not quite. The dreams of losing something precious in the fog had been a part of her for too long.

Just before she thought she might die from wanting him, she pulled away. Running a shaky hand through her hair, she stepped back and looked up at him.

"I'm sorry about the party, Todd. I'm sorry about . . . everything." She turned from him and ran up the stairs. She didn't think she could keep her resolve for one more minute.

The tears didn't come until she was inside her apartment. "I'm not going to cry," she said fiercely as the first fat droplets spilled down her face. She went into her bathroom and scrubbed her face. "I won't cry. I will forget him." But still the tears came. They trickled out, one by one, as Amy realized her loss.

She wiped the tears away with the back of her hand and dressed for bed. Just before she turned out the light, she noticed her little robot standing in the corner. "Why can't real people be restored with new circuits and new batteries, Herman?"

He made no reply, but stood solidly in the corner. Amy knew that it was within her power to keep Herman with her always.

On Tuesday she tried not to think about Todd and his party. She arose early and hurried to her perpetual popcorn popper, hoping to lose herself in her invention. But the scattered parts had lost their appeal. She stared down at them for thirty minutes without having one single brilliant idea. The only thing that came to mind was the way Todd's hand had felt on her leg as he had helped himself to her popcorn last night.

Not to be daunted, she embarked on a massive cleaning spree. Even Aunt Syl was impressed at the amount of dust Amy sent flying around the apartment.

"My, my. A body needs a mask and goggles to pass through here." Aunt Syl was, in fact, dressed in her new silver and pink wig and enormous sunglasses.

Amy looked up from her cleaning. "Going somewhere, Aunt Syl?"

"Out," she said mysteriously.

Amy laughed. "I see you're going incognito."

"I can't be bothered with adoring fans today. I have important things to do. Have fun rearranging our dust, dear."

Amy watched Aunt Syl leave, then attacked the apartment once more. She hummed as she worked, telling herself that she couldn't be so cheerful if her heart was broken. What did it matter if she never felt rainbows and magic again? she asked herself as she swept behind the sofa. She had Aunt Syl and Herman and Hortense. She didn't need somebody else to complicate her life.

She got a mop from the closet and waxed the old wooden floors until they squeaked. Her mind continued to whirl and spin. Suppose she had said yes to Todd? Could she count on his always being there? He loved boating. How did she know he wouldn't end up at the bottom of the Chesapeake?

By late afternoon she was exhausted. She showered and dressed in cool white cotton cropped pants and a sailor top. After tying her hair back with a bright blue ribbon, she went into the kitchen, still believing she could forget Todd by keeping busy.

She probably ranked among the world's ten worst cooks, but that didn't stop her. The countertops were soon covered with the makings of a Black Forest cake. Halfway through the cake, she decided that cooking was a mistake. Every time she stirred, she thought of Todd—laughing in his pristine kitchen, remarking about her jiggling, squeezing the egg rolls. With her mind more on the judge than on cooking, she created a lopsided confection held together with whipped cream and cherries.

Aunt Syl came in just as Amy was putting the last cherry on top.

"Are we having a party?" Aunt Syl asked.

"No."

"Then I think we should."

"Why?"

"Because it's Tuesday and somebody somewhere is having a birthday. I think we should help them celebrate."

Amy smiled. Aunt Syl could always make her smile, she thought, no matter how blue she felt. "We don't have any horns and bazookas."

Aunt Syl patted her cheek. "That's better. I knew you could smile if you tried. Now"—she adjusted her crooked wig—"I'm taking you to a lovely restaurant I discovered."

"I really don't feel like going out."

"I promise that we won't talk about that remarkable judge and why you've sent him away.

We won't discuss a thing except the price of sugar and Santa Claus."

"I do have to eat," Amy conceded.

"Good. And when we come back, I want you to die on the windowsill."

Amy laughed. "Again?"

"Feetfirst this time."

Aunt Syl was as good as her word. Dinner was a pleasant meal with no heart-wrenching discussions. When they returned to the apartment that evening, they were still laughing over a story Aunt Syl had told about Hortense in New York.

"And now," she said to Amy, "are you ready to die?"

"Tonight?" Amy asked. "You can't see me in the dark."

"I'll shine a flashlight down. Indulge me, dear. I'll get the rope."

"Rope?"

"You're hanging feetfirst, remember?" At Amy's look of alarm she added hastily, "I asked Justin how to do this. We'll tie the rope around the sofa leg and I'll lower you out the window. After I've seen one good scream or two, I'll pull you back up. Don't worry."

"Are you sure you can pull me back up?"

"Justin rigged a pulley for me. Don't worry."

Amy still had misgivings. "You keep saying that, but somehow it doesn't reassure me. I may be getting too old for these schemes of yours, Aunt Syl. I don't like this one."

"Trust me, dear. You'll like it." Aunt Syl smiled mysteriously, and the two of them set about rigging Amy for dying.

With one end of the rope securely around the sofa leg and the other end around her waist, Amy was lowered out the window. She held the window ledge as long as possible, then at Aunt Syl's coaxing let go. As she swung freely in the summer night, she decided it wasn't a bad way to spend an evening. It beat mourning over Todd.

"That's wonderful, dear," Aunt Syl called down. "Now I can tell just how the body falls."

"Great. Pull me back up."

"Not yet. I want to lower you just a fraction more."

Amy started laughing at the ludicrous situation. "To think I came all the way from Mississippi to die like this." She laughed even harder. "Lower away, Aunt Syl. I had nothing else to do this evening except go to the White House for a presidential reception."

"That's my girl." Aunt Syl lowered the rope so that Amy's legs were dangling outside the window of the apartment directly below them. "Telephone, dear. Don't go away. I'll be right back."

"Where would I go?" Amy asked. She swung in the dark, waiting for Aunt Syl to pull her back up. Music from the first-floor apartment was wafting around her in the night air. She hummed along with the lively jazz tune, then suddenly stiffened. Party music, she thought. She was dangling outside *Todd's* apartment.

"Aunt Syl," she called. "Pull me up."

There was no answer. Amy listened but she couldn't hear a thing.

"Aunt Syl," she called again. Still no answer. She groaned. Aunt Syl had probably forgotten all about her. Most likely she was now at her typewriter, pecking away while her inspiration was fresh.

Amy caught the rope with her hands and attempted to climb up it. Her effort caused her feet to tap against Todd's window. Quickly she ceased moving, hoping nobody inside would notice. She held her breath, then expelled it with a whoosh. Apparently the party was in full swing and nobody was paying any attention to the dilemma outside the window.

So much for Todd's vows of undying affection, she fumed as she struggled with the rope once more. All it took was one good party to wipe her completely from his mind. Her legs did a small cha-cha as she yanked angrily on the rope.

She'd show him. Why should she moon around when he seemed to be having so much fun? She'd cut her Black Forest cake and have a party of her own. She'd invite all her neighbors. Why, she'd even call Mrs. Matilda Hildenbrand.

The more Amy struggled, the madder she got. But she was no match for the rope. Hard as she tried, she couldn't pull herself up.

"This is a pretty pickle you've gotten yourself into," she muttered.

Suddenly the window below her flew open. Todd stuck his head out and grinned up at her.

"I see you've decided to join the party after all," he said.

"I'm not joining your party," she snapped.

"Then what are you doing?" His eyes were level with her bare calves. He thought the scenery outside his window had vastly improved.

"I'm sight-seeing," she said. "Baltimore by night." His face was so close to her legs, she could feel his breath. In spite of her anger, she tingled deliciously.

"What a remarkable idea," he said. "Do you mind if I join you?" He reached out and caught her legs.

She kicked against him. "Let go of me. You seem to have enough to occupy your time."

He didn't let go. "The party?" Tightening his hold, he let his other hand roam freely up and down her legs. "I would keep you here all night except that my brothers are waiting to meet you."

"Waiting? How did you know I'd be here?"

"Justin."

"And my Aunt Syl." She tried to be furious, but Todd was still caressing her legs. The best she could manage was a small scowl. And even that was hard. What she really wanted to do was swing outside his apartment all night and let him rub her legs. She decided she might even take up dangling from ropes as a hobby.

"And your Aunt Syl," he said, and reluctantly stopped his sensuous exploration of her legs.

With his hand off her legs, Amy could think again. "You knew about this all along? Why didn't you stop them?"

"It was too late." He leaned far out the window so he could reach up and circle Amy's upper thighs. "I'm going to get you down now, love. Untie the knot at your waist."

"I'd just as soon swing here until Aunt Syl repents and pulls me back up." She didn't know how she managed to say that with his face pressing against the front of her legs.

"This is no time to be stubborn. You might get hurt."

"You should have thought of that before you cooked up this scheme."

"I'm not going to respond to that false accusation until I get you down. Unite that knot," he demanded. "Trust me. I won't drop you." His arms tightened around her.

Hesitantly she did his bidding. Secure in his grip, she loosened the knot and put her hands on his shoulders. He carefully let her slide downward in his arms until he had her around the waist. Her feet were now touching the windowsill.

"Bend down, Amy, and I'll pull you in."

"You can let go now."

"Never."

He pulled her inside.

"I'll leave you to your schemes now," she said when her feet were safely on the floor.

He jerked her roughly against his chest. "I would never have been a party to such a scheme. Justin and your aunt planned the whole thing. You were already out the window when Justin confided in me. Aunt Syl would have loved that scene. It was almost murder for real. He swore in blood that the rope and pulley were safe." Todd buried his face in her hair. "You feel so good. It seems like years since Sunday."

It did to Amy also, but she wasn't about to confess that to Todd. Hadn't she spent the last two days trying to get him out of her mind, out of her heart? No matter how good his arms felt, she was determined to put him out of her life.

"Nothing has changed, Todd," she said quietly. "Please let go."

He released her immediately. "At least meet my brothers before you go."

"What's the point?"

He saw the stubborn tilt of her chin, the remoteness in her blue eyes. He felt helpless against the barrier she had erected between them. If she had put a name to her fear, he could have dealt with it. But she refused to name it and he could only guess. He suspected its name was Death, that grim reaper that had prematurely claimed both her parents and her husband. Her dream had been the biggest clue.

A longing to shield her welled up inside him, to protect her from everything bad that would ever happen. He reached for her again, then let his hand drop without touching her. Now was not the time to press, he decided. Dangling from a rope was enough trauma for one evening. Dammit, he'd pretend to be lighthearted even if the effort killed him.

He smiled. "The point, love, is that my brothers have never met an inventor."

She caught her lower lip between her teeth in momentary indecision, then smiled. "All right. Just this once. I'll meet them—as an inventor and nothing more."

"Agreed."

Ten

Amy hadn't meant to be enchanted by Todd's family. She had never intended to stay beyond the first hello. But now she stood in the middle of the party, surrounded by three men who were as charming as they were good-looking. Todd's brothers seemed to be trying to outdo one another in claiming her attention. They asked her about her inventions and regaled her with funny stories of their childhood escapades. She laughed so much she completely forgot she was suffering from a broken heart.

Todd beamed at them from across the room. "There's nothing like having reinforcements," he said as Justin passed by with an open bottle of champagne.

"I've discovered that cupid often needs assistance, sir," Justin said.

"Right. But don't you and Aunt Syl get any more ideas. I still haven't forgiven you for the rope and pulley trick."

"All's well that ends well," Justin said.

Todd laughed. "It hasn't ended yet. Serve the champagne, Shakespeare."

As Justin moved away, Todd's attention returned to Amy. She was so interested in the pictures Jeff was showing that she automatically lifted her glass for a refill when Justin paused beside her. Todd smiled at her animated face. He knew what the pictures were. He figured he'd seen them no less than a hundred times. Jeff was the Cunningham family's proud papa. His brothers teased him about carrying so many family photographs in his pockets. They often said he would soon have to take a wheelbarrow around to haul his pictures.

Todd eased closer as Jeff's wife, Bonnie, a vivacious blonde, joined the group. He was irresistibly drawn to Amy's glowing face as she talked about the family pictures.

"Such beautiful children!" he heard her exclaim.

"I won't argue with you," Jeff said. "My four kids have to be the smartest, handsomest kids in Baltimore."

Bonnie took Jeff's arm and gave him an adoring smile. "Listen to the proud papa talk." Turning to Amy, she said, "You have to take what he says with a grain of salt. He's prejudiced."

Amy scanned the photographs again. There were three boys and one girl, ranging from age twelve all the way down to three. The oldest boy had flaming red hair, but the three other children were dark-haired, blue-eyed replicas of Jeff.

"His hair is gorgeous," Amy said as she pointed to the twelve-year-old's picture. "It reminds me of a sunset."

"He has his father's hair," Bonnie said.

Startled, Amy looked at Jeff's dark curls.

"My first husband," Bonnie explained. "He was

killed when Ricky was three. Ricky also inherited his freckles."

"But he has his dad's sparkling personality," Jeff said.

Bonnie laughed and pinched his cheek. "And his big ego."

Amy glanced in confusion from one to the other. How could all this love and laughter have come out of tragedy? she wondered. What had given Bonnie the courage to risk loving again?

Todd walked quietly up behind her and slipped an arm around her shoulders. "It's remarkable what marriage can do to a man," he said. "You should have seen Jeff in his bachelor days. He had the name of every woman in Baltimore in his little black book. Mike and Wayne and I thought he would never tie the knot."

"And now we're thinking the same thing about you, Todd," Mike added.

"Damn right," Wayne said. "Isn't that a gray hair I see near your temple?"

Jeff punched Todd's arm. "You ought to try it, old man. There's nothing like finding your only pair of clean socks being used to plug up a hole in the magazine basket."

"Are you complaining?" Bonnie asked.

"Who me?" Jeff was the picture of innocence. "You know I prefer to wear my shoes without socks. It adds a little pizzazz to my life."

Bonnie turned to Amy. "He gets like this when he's hungry. Let me feed him before he really says something crazy." The two of them walked toward the buffet, smiling at each other as if they had a million private jokes between them.

"Food. That's a great idea," Wayne said. "Follow that couple, Mike." They left Amy and Todd alone.

Todd squeezed Amy's shoulders. "What do you think of my brothers?"

Amy knew she should leave. She knew she should remove Todd's arm. But staying felt good and his arm was like heaven. Unconsciously she moved closer to him. "I think your brothers are terrific. And so is Bonnie."

Todd's heart did a riotous fandango as he noticed her moves. "They have great ideas too."

"Todd," she said warningly.

"All right. I promise to be good." He leaned down and nuzzled her neck.

"You call that being good?"

"Yes. I didn't promise to be a saint. Only a saint could be around you and resist touching you."

She knew she should pull away, but she couldn't. She blamed it on the champagne. She knew she should go, but she didn't have the will. She blamed it on the party atmosphere.

A gaiety filled her spirit as she looked up at Todd. For the moment, all her reasons for resisting him were forgotten.

"Nobody loves a saint," she said.

"What about a judge?"

Her breath caught in her throat. "Some people find them tolerable."

"Are inventors among that group?"

"I really couldn't say."

"Why not?"

"My head is filled with champagne bubbles. I can't think straight."

"Then I'll do the thinking for both of us. Wait right here while I get you some food."

"I have to go."

"No, you don't." He maneuvered her into a chair and joined the group at the buffet.

A distinguished-looking gray-haired man approached Amy. Smiling, he sat in the chair beside her. "You must be Amy Logan." He held out a slim hand. "I'm Randall Crane, an associate of Todd's."

Amy liked the man immediately. He had a frank and friendly manner that made talking with him easy. "Yes, I'm Amy Logan. How did you know?"

"Todd has described you perfectly. Besides, you have a certain notoriety around the courthouse since your last appearance with Mrs. Hildenbrand."

Amy laughed. "That was the highlight of my disturbing-the-peace career."

A tall woman with burnished silver hair joined them. She crossed her slim legs as she sat beside them. "I see Randall has found you. He's been dying to meet you ever since you brought your robot into Todd's courtroom. He says nothing like that ever happens in his courtroom." When she smiled, a fine network of lines radiated from her hazel eyes. "Hi. I'm Joyce, Randall's better half."

"A statement I'll not dispute, my dear." Randall smiled fondly at his wife.

Amy was so enthralled with the lovely couple that she didn't even notice Todd until she felt his hand on her shoulder. Something inside her melted at his touch. Even though he was standing behind her so that she couldn't see his face, she would have known his hand if a dozen others had been touching her. It felt solid and warm. It felt like a promise.

Joyce smiled up at Todd. "You must bring Amy to visit us, Todd. I want to hear all about her inventions and her famous aunt. And I especially want to know how she got up enough courage to make a shambles out of the orderly Judge Cunningham's courtroom. Nobody's ever done that before."

"I wouldn't call it a shambles," Todd said.

"Oh, dear," Amy said. "Did I ruin his reputation?"

"On the contrary," Randall assured her. "You added a little spice to his image. Sometimes we judges are considered to be colorless old relics hiding in our dusty robes."

Joyce patted her husband's cheek. "You're far from colorless, dear." Turning to Amy, she said, "Remind me to tell you about the time he stuck a toothpick in his cigar so that he could mesmerize the jury with an ash that wouldn't fall off."

Amy laughed. "I'd love to hear about that."

Joyce stood, pulling her husband up with her. "We've monopolized you long enough. I do believe Todd's going to mutilate that poor snack plate he's holding if we don't leave you two alone."

"She's a wise and brilliant woman," Todd said as he sat in Joyce's vacated chair. "Have a shrimp." He outlined Amy's lips with a fingertip as he held the shrimp toward her.

"I really shouldn't." Considering that his finger had set her mouth on fire, it was a miracle she could speak. "I have to be going."

But she didn't go. She ate the shrimp . . . and the liver pâté and the cheese straws and the strawberries big enough to pass as apples. She drank the champagne and talked to the people. She learned that the man who lived next door to her always had a secret yen to own a robot, and she promised to demonstrate Herman for him. She made friends with her across-the-hall neighbor, the one who had charged her with disturbing the peace. She even charmed the old sourpuss who lived across from Todd, and who espoused the philosophy that the whole world was going to hell in a handbasket.

And always, there was Todd. Whether he was beside her, touching her shoulder, leaning down to whisper into her ear, or was across the room from her, sending signals with his remarkable eyes, she was always aware of his presence.

She didn't want the party to end. She wanted to shut out the real world and live forever in the security and gaiety of Todd's apartment. She wanted to bottle the laughter and the joy. She wanted to keep the bright lights and the music going, the champagne flowing. But most of all, she wanted to hold Todd at her side forever.

Amy stayed until all the guests were gone. She was slightly tipsy on champagne and totally drunk on love. But she wouldn't have admitted it if grizzly bears had been threatening her.

Todd was across the room, showing the last guest out. She smiled crookedly at him and tried to think how she might get upstairs without falling victim to his charm. Her legs went weak as he came toward her. All he needed to do, she decided, was crook his finger and she would go flying into his arms. She would love him one more time, and then she would get on with the painful business of putting him out of her life.

He didn't crook his finger. He knelt beside her chair and took her hand. "Thank you for staying, Amy."

She resisted the urge to reach out and touch his hair. "I'm a weak character. I took the easy way out. Going would have taken more courage than staying."

"You're not weak; you're strong."

"Not like Bonnie."

"No. Not like Bonnie. Each person is different, Amy. Everybody handles tragedy in his own way.

Some, like Bonnie, reach out to others while some have to go through the healing process alone."

Amy squeezed his hand. Even if she couldn't marry Todd, she thought he was probably the best friend she would ever have. "When I put away the paintings, I thought the healing was complete."

"It was so far as Tim is concerned, but you've lost more than a husband. I think you never came to terms with losing your parents."

"I did. I had Aunt Syl. I had a happy childhood."

"I don't dispute that. Your dream gave me the clue, though. I think you're afraid to risk loving and losing again."

"Then why are you bothering with me? Why don't you find somebody who isn't afraid?"

"Because I intend to break through that barrier you've put up. I intend to confront your old dragon, fear, and slay it."

She giggled. "I never knew judges were dragon slayers."

"Judges are many things, including gallant knights." He lifted her from her chair. "And to show you how gallant I am, I'm taking you back to your apartment instead of into my bedroom where you belong."

Her knees went weak at the thought of his bedroom. She knew how the room would look in the moonlight. She knew exactly how the sheets would feel. She knew precisely how Todd's head would look on the pillow next to hers.

She gave him an enigmatic smile. "Is that gallantry or fear? Perhaps you're afraid I'll say no again."

He was delighted with her comeback. "Perhaps I am. Why don't you do a little dragon slaying of your own?"

"Not tonight. I'm fresh out of dragon bait."

Todd didn't know how he managed to get her out of his apartment without giving in to temptation. He didn't know how he was able to climb up the stairs behind her without grabbing her. All he knew was that he was finally standing outside her door and he couldn't let her go.

As she put her hand on the doorknob, he took her shoulders and turned her back around.

"Something to keep the dragons away," he said. His lips captured hers in a long, searching kiss.

His mouth demanded. Hungrily.

She responded. Willingly.

His tongue plundered.

She moaned.

He hauled her hips against his and began a grinding, erotic rhythm. Her hands tangled in his hair as she strained to get even closer. Fire skittered along her nerve endings and inflamed her body. The heat rushed through her, hotter than a summer wind, more intense than the summer sun.

His body commanded.

She obeyed.

His hips led.

She followed.

And when it seemed they might stay locked together in the darkened hallway forever, their bodies went limp.

"I like the way you chase dragons, Judge."

"If they bother you tonight, give me a call. You should see my technique for putting them to rout in a bedroom."

"I already have. Good night, Todd."

"Good night, Amy," he said as she slipped inside her apartment.

He stood in the empty hallway for a full two minutes before leaving. His breathing was ragged and his heart was pumping full blast. As he looked at her closed door, he vowed that he would tear down her walls of fear, even if it took the rest of his life.

Inside her apartment, Amy leaned against her door. She knew Todd was still out there. She could feel his presence. She put her hand over her heart, trying to calm its erratic rhythm. If she had been confused Sunday, she thought, she was thoroughly bewildered now. How could she resolve to forget Todd, then go so willingly into his arms? How could she vow to put him out of her life forever, then kiss him as if she would never let go?

She was tempted to open the door and invite him in. She was tempted to let him examine her dragons, label them and slay them, one by one. Could he? Or was that something she had to do herself?

At last she heard his footsteps in the hall. The moment for exploring fears had passed. It was just as well, she decided. After swinging from her window by a rope and drinking two glasses of champagne, she was in no condition to slay mice, let alone dragons.

Amy slept late on Wednesday. When she awoke, Aunt Syl was in the kitchen surrounded by pots and pans.

"Good morning, dear," Aunt Syl said cheerfully. "I'm cooking breakfast. Pancakes."

"You're *cooking*?"

"It's a peace offering. To make up for the rope and pulley."

"Nothing can make up for that trick, Aunt Syl."

Amy's smile spoiled the intended effect of her words.

Aunt Syl didn't miss a thing. Not the smile or the softening of the face or the sparkling eyes. "I can see how upset you are. How was the party?"

"Fine."

"There's a thesaurus on my desk, Amy. Run in there and see if you can't come up with something more descriptive. Fabulous. Extraordinary. Fantastic. Mind-boggling. Londerful."

"Londerful?"

"A combination of love and wonderful."

Amy poured herself a cup of tea and sat at the table. "Now, Aunt Syl, just because I was forced to attend that party, don't think I've changed my mind about anything else."

"Did I say anything?"

"No. But I know what you were thinking."

"When did you take up mind reading?"

"About the same time you took up matchmaking."

Aunt Syl laughed. "I enjoyed it. I may give up mystery writing and go into matchmaking full-time. Sort of like Dolly Levi. What do you think, Amy?"

"I don't think Broadway is ready for you."

Aunt Syl turned back to her cooking. "Balderdash!" she said as she looked into her mixing bowl. "Have you ever seen pancake batter that turned purple and bubbled?"

Amy walked over to the counter and peered over Aunt Syl's shoulder. The purple pancake batter was bubbling happily in the bowl. "What did you put in it?"

"You know those wonderful blueberry pancakes on the waterfront?" Amy nodded. "Well," Aunt Syl continued, "I didn't have blueberries so I put in grapes."

"Is that all?"

"Well, let me see now . . ." Aunt Syl scanned the littered countertops. "There's flour and eggs and sugar and a pinch of soda . . . maybe more than a pinch." Her face brightened. "Oh, yes, I added a little wine for good measure."

Amy picked up the empty bottle. "A *little* wine?"

"Maybe more than a little . . . enough to taste."

Amy laughed. "I think I'll have cereal this morning." As she got the milk from the refrigerator, she said over her shoulder, "Remind me not to let you make my wedding cake."

She didn't notice her slip of the tongue, but Aunt Syl did. Smiling brightly, she dipped a spoon into the pancake batter and lifted it to her lips. "Ummm. Not bad, even if I do say so myself."

Amy smiled about the purple pancake batter all day. At least she told herself that was why she was smiling. She felt so good she almost finished her perpetual popcorn popper.

Todd called that night.

"Seen any dragons lately, love?" he asked.

"Only Aunt Syl's purple pancake batter." She told him the story of their would-be breakfast.

Todd laughed, and they talked of inconsequential things—the weather, the movies, the next outdoor concert. They skirted around the real issues of love already declared and marriage denied and fears not faced.

After they hung up, Amy was vaguely dissatisfied. She prowled around the apartment, selected and rejected three books, and finally ended up leaning on the windowsill looking out across the darkened Bay. The fragrance from her multi-colored petunias wafted around her.

"You are my rainbow, Todd," she said softly as she lowered her face to the blossoms.

Later that night she dreamed of reaching for Todd through the fog. She could almost feel the damp chill on her face as she stretched her hand through the cotton-wool blur that obscured him. Suddenly her hand closed around something solid. Todd's hand. She caught it and held on. In her dream she clung to him. Although his face was lost in the fog, his hand was always there.

Thursday evening Todd sent roses and an invitation to dinner. Amy declined.

When Justin returned with her note, Todd questioned him.

"How did she look, Justin? Was she cheerful? Was she rested?"

Justin laughed. "A body would think you hadn't seen her in three years. Why don't you go upstairs and see for yourself?"

"I'll wait. She'll call to thank me for the flowers."

Todd glanced at the clock. What was Amy doing now? he wondered. Was she smelling the roses and thinking of him?

He prowled his immaculate apartment, waiting for the phone to ring. He put a jazz tape on and flipped through the latest issue of *U.S. News and World Report*. From time to time he glanced toward the phone, but it remained silent.

He threw the magazine aside and stared out the window. How long would it take Amy to realize that life was full of risks? he wondered. How long would it take her to see that some things were worth the risk? Maybe giving her so much time was a mistake. Maybe she was using the time to put him out of her mind rather than to resolve her fears. Maybe he should give fate another little push.

He reached for the phone, then withdrew his hand. Dammit. What did he think he could do? Carry her to the altar kicking and screaming? There were some things Amy had to decide for herself.

He stalked into his pristine kitchen and poured himself a tall glass of lemonade. It was cool and slightly tart, with pulp from real lemons floating in the glass. But it was not refreshing. Todd sat glumly at his spotless table and decided nothing would ever refresh him again.

Taking his glass, he walked through his apartment, hoping to feel that familiar surge of pleasure the orderliness of his dwelling always gave him. Instead, he imagined a bawdy-tongued parrot swinging from a chandelier and a woman with a China doll face standing in the midst of a cluttered workroom.

He slammed his glass so hard against a marble-topped table, the ice rattled. "Dammit," he muttered. "She could have at least called about the roses."

When the phone rang, he nearly knocked over a chair getting to it. It turned out to be his brother Jeff.

"It's you," Todd said.

"What do you mean, it's me? Were you expecting somebody else? Amy, maybe?" Jeff's voice dripped good cheer, and, as usual, he got right to the point.

"Why would I be expecting Amy to call?" Todd

asked testily. "She made her policy of no commitments perfectly clear in the beginning. Anybody would need to have his head examined for sending roses to press a hopeless case."

"Uh-oh. The woman's playing hard to get."

"Dammit. She's not playing. She's running scared and I'm getting senile for being a sentimental fool." Todd scowled at his glass; it was sweating a puddle on his immaculate table. "My life was perfectly satisfactory before she came to Baltimore. I don't know why I would want somebody like her anyway."

"Like what?"

"She doesn't know the meaning of order. Her apartment looks like she's getting ready for a rummage sale, and she never has anything in her refrigerator except wilted lettuce."

"That's just what you need, brother. Somebody to put a little zip in your life."

"If I want zip, I'll have Justin add Tabasco to my tomato juice."

After he had hung up, Todd hugged his righteous anger to himself, thinking the remark about Tabasco proved he could handle anything, even losing Amy.

After she had sent Justin away, Amy put her roses in water and spent the next fifteen minutes moving them around her apartment. She wanted them to be in exactly the right spot, so she could see them no matter where she was. She thought of dividing the bouquet and putting each rose in a bud vase, one in every corner of the apartment. But then she wouldn't be able to pass by and smell the delicious fragrance of the whole bouquet. She finally put them beside her favorite chair.

She sat down, letting their sweet smell wash over her. From time to time she glanced at the phone. He would surely call, she thought. Hadn't he vowed to break down her barriers? Hadn't he promised to slay her dragons?

The silent phone mocked her. Maybe she should call him. Maybe she should let him know that she had found him in her fog dream. At least she should thank him for the roses. She reached for the phone, then withdrew her hand. Was the dream important? Did it mean she was willing to risk losing someone she loved again? Could she marry Todd and not be haunted by the fear that he would be taken from her? Her mind tried to recapture the forlornness of death, but the smell of roses got in the way.

She plucked a blossom from the vase. Its delicate beauty was like a promise. She held it to her face. Tomorrow would be soon enough to think about the future. She placed the rose on her pillow when she went to bed.

Late Friday afternoon Jeff stopped by to visit his brother.

"Bonnie and I thought we'd have the two of you over for dinner tomorrow night." Jeff tried to make the invitation sound casual, as if he and his wife hadn't been hatching an elaborate matchmaking scheme.

Todd didn't have to ask who the other person was. Amy. Just thinking her name brought a hollow feeling to the pit of his stomach. Another whole day had gone by, and he still had not heard

from her. "Forget it," he said. "The lady's surrounded herself by a wall of silence. What makes
you think a dinner invitation will break it down?"

Jeff didn't lose his good cheer. He plopped onto
the sofa and stretched his long legs in front of
him. "Love has made you surly."

"It'll pass."

"What? The love or the surliness?"

"Both."

"One thing you have to know about love, brother,
is that you can't sentence it like a criminal and
expect it to disappear onto the top shelf of the
closet."

Todd's grunt passed for laughter. "Your meta-
phors stink."

"What do you expect from an engineer?" Jeff
rose. "Dinner's at eight."

He was out the door before Todd could say he
wouldn't be there.

Amy was flabbergasted when Todd's brother
showed up at her apartment. She was even more
aghast when he invited her to Saturday night
dinner.

"Well, of course, I can't go," she said.

"Why not?"

"Because . . ." She couldn't think of anything
else to say.

"Don't you eat?"

"Yes."

"It's settled then. Bonnie will pick you up at
seven-thirty."

He was gone before she could say no.

*   *   *

All day Saturday, Amy tried to put Todd out of her mind, but every time she looked at the roses she felt such weak-kneed desire, she had to sit down. "I really should throw them into the trash can," she muttered on more than one occasion.

At least five times during the day she reached for the phone to call Bonnie and politely decline the dinner invitation. Visions of Todd always stopped her, though—the way he looked in the sailboat with the wind in his hair, the way his smile went crooked and dreamy when they made love, the way he squeezed her hand in response to her unspoken need.

By late afternoon she was exhausted from the effort of indecision and feelings of frustration. When the hands of the clock approached six, she showered and shampooed her hair. "I must be crazy," she mumbled as she dried off.

Afterward she tried on and rejected three dresses. "Of course I'm not going," she muttered. "I will not be manipulated this way." She smoothed her slip over her slim hips and reached into her closet for a green silk dress. The full skirt billowed as she slipped it over her head. "This is another of Todd's schemes to make me change my mind." She struggled with the zipper as she talked. "If he thinks having dinner with his brother's family will make me change my mind, he's sadly mistaken."

The green silk swirled around her legs as she paced the floor. What was she going to do? She should have called Jeff and Bonnie immediately to say she couldn't come. What had stopped her? Was she so weak that she constantly let other people manipulate her, or was she so in love that she let her heart rule her head? She didn't even want to think about that possibility. Nobody could be that much in love. She had to be practical. She had to remember that the pain of loving and losing was too great to risk again.

She glanced at the clock. Seven. Too late to call and cancel now. Bonnie would have made dinner preparations. Not going would be unthinkable. Amy sighed. What was she going to do about this dilemma?

She sat down at her dressing table and carefully applied her makeup. The only thing to do was make the best of a bad situation, she decided. Perhaps she could even use this opportunity to make it perfectly clear to Todd that she had no intention of changing her mind. At that thought, her loneliness almost overwhelmed her. She leaned her head on her hands and took a big, gulping breath. Why didn't life come with guarantees?

Lifting her head, she finished her makeup, then walked carefully into the sitting room as if any unnecessary movement might shatter her resolve.

"Aunt Syl," she called, "I'm going out to dinner."

Aunt Syl emerged from her room, trailing a shocking pink feather boa and pushing at her topsy-turvy matching wig. "Wonderful, dear. With Todd, I hope. It's time to quit this silly cat-and-mouse game."

"This is not a game, Aunt Syl; it's my life. Everybody seems to keep forgetting that."

"I'll admit to being brash and pushy about this romance. One of the perks of being my age is that you can do and say anything you like and nobody dares reprimand you for fear you'll die and they'll feel guilty."

Amy chuckled. "Aunt Syl, you're impossible."

"But adorable, don't you think?"

"Positively."

Bonnie and Jeff lived in a charming Georgian home that overlooked the Bay. Huge cascades of summer flowers spilled over polished tabletops, and the delicious yeasty aroma of home-baked bread filled the air. Children's laughter echoed down the stairway, and Jeff outdid himself in being gracious.

The cheerful, homey atmosphere caught Amy off guard. She found it impossible to remain cool and detached. By the time Todd arrived, she was engaged in a lively debate with Jeff about the impact of robots on industry.

When Todd entered the room, her sentence trailed into nothingness, and the subject of robots skittered completely out of her mind. He stood in the doorway, bronzed and handsome, filling her vision. He must have said something to Bonnie and Jeff, for his lips were moving, but Amy heard nothing except the symphony of her own heart.

He walked toward her, his lips curved into the merest suggestion of a smile, his eyes locked on hers. "Amy," he said in that wonderful drums and cymbals voice. She wondered if her legs would continue to hold her up.

"Todd." She hoped he wouldn't try to touch her. If he touched her, she might make a fool of herself in front of his family. She might wrap herself in his arms and stay there forever.

Her sigh of relief was audible when he stopped inches away.

"How are you?" His question was polite, re-

mote, as if they were nothing more than acquain-
tances.

"Fine," she said aloud. Lonesome, she said to
herself. Vulnerable. Scared. Uncertain.

They stood facing each other, both desperate to
reach out and touch, both clinging to a fragile
thread of self-control. The fragrance of summer
flowers drifted around them unappreciated, and
the hall clock chimed eight unnoticed.

Their forgotten hosts exchanged a significant
look. "Why don't we go into the dining room?"
Jeff said. "Bonnie's made her specialty."

Todd shrugged his shoulders as if throwing off
a magic spell and turned to his brother. "Corned
beef?" he asked. He was grateful for this new
topic of conversation—food. He was grateful for
anything that kept him from forgetting that Amy
was out of his reach, shut up behind her wall of
fear.

"With cabbage and potatoes," Jeff added. He
took Amy's arm. "I have to watch my brother. If
he didn't have Justin, I'm afraid he'd take Bonnie
away from me simply because of her cooking."

"How did he get Justin?" Amy asked, but only
half-listened as Jeff told her how Justin had answered Todd's classified ad for a housekeeper. As
they walked to the dining room she was vividly
aware of Todd walking behind her, of his gaze on
her. The back of her neck tingled. She felt breathless and flushed. This was no way to forget a
man, she thought. And she knew she shouldn't
have come.

Conversation during dinner was strained. Amy
and Todd went to elaborate lengths to avoid talking directly to each other, while Jeff and Bonnie
made valiant efforts to bring them together. Over

dessert Amy decided that it had been the longest meal in the history of eating.

Bonnie looked around the table and gave everybody a forced smile. "Jeff is going to help me make coffee. Why don't you show Amy the rose garden, Todd?"

Amy wanted to scream. Since when did it take two to make coffee? She looked down at her empty plate as if she found the cake crumbs fascinating.

"Certainly," Todd said.

He came around the table and pulled back her chair. A shock went through her as his hands touched her bare arm. Was it deliberate?

"Thank you," she said, then almost groaned aloud. She sounded like one of her own robots.

Barely touching her elbow, Todd led her outside. The brick patio was softly lit by the moon and outdoor lanterns. An informal rose garden flanked its south side.

"Bonnie has thirty-five varieties of roses," Todd said. "She started this rose garden right after she and Jeff married." He ached to take Amy into his arms. He longed to kiss her until she forgot about death and pain and loss. But he wouldn't barge across the barriers she had erected.

Amy walked away from him and knelt beside a bush that was ablaze with fiery red roses. She pressed her face into a flower and closed her eyes. How long could she hold herself aloof from him? she wondered. Could she keep her resolve until she returned to the safe haven of her apartment? Maybe if she kept her face buried in the rose, he'd go away. She was so still she could almost hear the moon tracking across the sky.

Todd continued. "Bonnie knows more about aphids and black rose blight than anybody in

Baltimore. She calls last summer the summer of the snail. Jeff says she spent more time out here battling the slimy things than she did with him."

Abruptly, Amy stood up. "Thank you." She almost reached for him, but she settled for a smile. It didn't feel as good as touching him, but it felt safe.

"For what?" he asked.

"For being my best friend. For talking about roses and aphids instead of—" She hesitated, watching her lower lip between her teeth.

"Dragons?"

"Yes."

"I want to. I want to make you put those fears aside. I want to force you to give your life a chance to happen."

"You can't. I'm the only person who can decide how to live my life."

"I know that." His blue gaze was so intense it seemed to burn right through her. "Dammit, Amy." He shoved his clenched fists into his pockets. "I've tried to be patient. I've even tried to be mad at you." In one swift movement he took his hands from his pockets and grabbed her shoulders. "I must be going crazy." He pulled her close, cupping the back of her head and cradling it against his chest.

She leaned against him, loving his strength, reveling in his nearness, grateful for his self-control.

They held on to each other for a small eternity. The heady scent of a thousand roses swirled around them, and the beams from the summer moon washed over them. It was a night made for romance.

To Bonnie and Jeff, peering out the window,

Amy and Todd might have been the perfect lovers. But they were fooled by appearances. They couldn't see the anguish of indecision, the turmoil of restraint. They couldn't see the shadows of the past, the misgivings about the future. In their blindness they turned from the window and congratulated each other on the success of their matchmaking scheme.

And on the patio, the forlorn lovers drew apart.

"Give us a chance, Amy," Todd said.

"I can't."

Todd remembered Amy's words as he gathered his dirty laundry one evening. It had been three days since the dinner, and he still had not heard from her. He was bleary-eyed from lack of sleep, and his usual good nature had been replaced by a snappishness that tried even Justin's patience.

He stomped down to the laundry room, taking a perverse satisfaction in the blistering heat. Why should he be comfortable? he wondered. He was miserable on the inside; he might as well be miserable on the outside too.

He slung his clothes into the machines willy-nilly, not caring whether he mixed colors with whites. As water began pouring into the machines, he sank into a chair and hunched over a legal tome. Sweat poured down the side of his face and dampened the front of his T-shirt. A mosquito buzzed around his head. He welcomed it too.

He tried to concentrate, but the words on the page blurred. He slammed the book shut and paced the room. He had always been a man of action, a man for whom decisions came easy, but Amy had him on the horns of a dilemma. As much as he wanted to have her, he knew he couldn't make her decisions for her. She had to come to terms with her past in her own way.

He sat back down and listened to the mechanical chugging of the machines.

Amy hadn't been able to work for three days. She felt helpless and frustrated. Instead of using the dinner to put Todd completely out of her life, she had used it to store up precious memories of him. What was she going to do? She had thought she couldn't risk loving and losing him, but she was beginning to think she couldn't live without him. If only she could talk to her best friend. But that was impossible. Her best friend was Todd.

She smiled sadly. Friend and lover. Were they one and the same, or could they be separated? She had to talk to him. She reached for the phone, then drew back her hand. It wouldn't be fair. She couldn't ask him to be an objective friend in a matter that also involved his heart.

The stifling heat seemed to be closing in on her. She had to get out of the apartment. It felt like a prison.

"Aunt Syl," she called. "I'm going out."

"On your way back, stop by the laundry room and get the tea towels out of the dryer. I forgot them."

The city of Baltimore was a heated blur. After only ten minutes of walking, Amy turned back to her apartment. Her thoughts were her jailer, not her dwelling. They had followed her down the streets, relentless in their pursuit. Should she reach out to Todd? Should she embrace life, as Aunt Syl always said, or shut herself away? Wasn't loneliness almost as painful as loss? Wasn't it a kind of death?

Her footsteps quickened as she neared the apartment building. She would talk to Todd. She would go to his apartment and talk to her best friend. The hallway felt cool after the outside heat. She pressed the buzzer to his apartment, waiting anxiously while the sound echoed in the empty rooms. She rang again, just to be certain, but he was not there.

She started toward the stairs, then remembered Aunt Syl's laundry. She changed her direction and took the back stairs down to the basement. As she neared it she could hear the clanging of the ancient, overworked machines.

The steam coming from the laundry room assaulted her face, and the man bending over the machines assaulted her heart. She clutched the doorjamb. "Todd."

He turned around, holding a soggy pink undershirt in his hand. Grinning, he said, "I put my whites in with Grandpa Tuck's red union suit."

Happy memories flooded over her. The early morning sunrise with Todd at her side, the kisses on the sandy beach. She laughed aloud. "Oh, Todd. The union suit." She crossed the room and took the pink T-shirt from him. "What am I going to do about you?" she asked softly.

"Marry me."

"Maybe. You persuade me." She held the wet T-shirt in front of her like a barrier, but this time Todd crossed over.

He bent swiftly, capturing her lips in a kiss edged with desperation. She opened her mouth to him hungrily. The kiss was wet and deep and soul-searching. It toppled barriers and reduced fears and slayed dragons. It confirmed what Amy was almost ready to admit: Life without Todd was no life at all.

He came up for air. "Come with me, Amy," he murmured into her ear. "Be my love."

She buried her face against his chest. "Not yet. Oh, please, not yet. This is too important. I must be very sure."

His hands caressed her back. "I know, love. I know. But don't be surprised if Justin kicks me out of the apartment while you're making up your mind."

"Out of your own apartment?"

"He's possessive about his work. He doesn't like bedroom slippers in the refrigerator and water rings on the coffee table."

She pulled out of his arms. "I'm afraid we're wet." She held up the T-shirt that had been scrunched between them. The fronts of both their shirts were damp and slightly pink.

Todd's eyes came unfocused as he looked down at her. Her shirt molded her breasts, showing her nipples peaked with arousal.

"Amy, a man can stand only so much temptation."

Her laugh was shaky. "I'm going."

He caught her hand. "If I don't hear from you soon, I'm liable to come break your door down."

"That would be disturbing the peace."

"That's all right. I know the judge."

She left before things got completely out of hand.

That night she lay in her bed thinking about her choices. She could continue to refuse Todd. She could live a careful life, making no commitments, taking no risks. She'd have her robot and Aunt Syl. And she would be lonely. Or she could reach out to Todd. She could have love and laughter and joy. She could have a rich and full life. But she would have no guarantees. Todd couldn't make those guarantees. Nobody could. Was she willing to take the risk?

The fog dream returned, but something was different. A bright shaft of sunlight burned the mists away, and she could see Todd clearly. She reached out her hand and he was there. Not just his hand, but all of him. In her dream she looked up into his face and smiled. It was a smile of affirmation.

The next day Amy was positively inspired. She whistled as she worked. If she kept up this pace, she thought, her perpetual popcorn popper would be finished by nightfall.

As she worked she thought of Todd. She thought of his wacky sense of humor, of the washtub boat and the union suit flag. She thought of his keen appreciation of nature, of the beauty of the sunset on the Chesapeake and the glory of the sunrise. She remembered his warmth, his way of touching her at unexpected times. And she knew without any shadow of doubt that she would risk anything—even the pain of loss—to be with him. Not just for a day or a week or a year, but as long as their forever lasted.

"Aunt Syl," she called. "Stir up some purple pancake batter. Get out your bazookas and tin drums. Put on your party wig."

Aunt Syl left her typewriter and fairly flew into the room. "What's all the excitement?"

"There's going to be a wedding."

"Hooray and hallelujah." She grabbed Amy and

twirled around the room. There was so much laughter and excitement, Hortense took refuge on the chandelier.

Suddenly Aunt Syl stopped dancing. "Does Todd know?"

"No. I haven't told him yet."

"My dear, don't you think he should know?"

"Yes. He should be back from court soon. I'll call him."

"Oh, my, no. That will never do."

"Why not?"

"Too unromantic. We must think of a plan," Aunt Syl said.

As Amy leaned out the window and watched for Todd, she began to have doubts about the plan. She really wouldn't blame Todd if he ran like a scared rabbit. She didn't know how she had let herself be talked into this. Aunt Syl had wisely departed from the scene of the crime, saying she would take in a long movie. Even her argument—that if Todd was going to be a part of the family he had better get used to craziness—was beginning to lose its appeal. Maybe she would call him after all, Amy thought.

She wandered over to her perpetual popcorn popper and aimlessly flipped it on. She was proud of her latest invention.

"Look at this, Herman," she said. She ran across the room and turned him on. "How can you look if nobody turns you on?"

The robot circled the room, seeming to beam approvingly at the popcorn popper.

Smiling, Amy returned to the window. Maybe she would go through with it after all, she thought.

She stared down at the sidewalk until she began to feel dizzy. Where was Todd?

Suddenly she saw him coming down the street. He was walking with that familiar jaunty self-confidence she loved so much. She was entranced with watching him and almost forgot about her plan. He was directly beneath her window when she remembered.

"Look out below!" she yelled.

She had waited too long. Instead of falling at his feet, the withered rose landed on his head, its petals cascading down his face. The rose was from the bouquet he had sent, the bouquet she hadn't been able to throw away even after all the petals had dried up.

He glanced up at the window. The nearly naked rose stem fell to the sidewalk. "I'm seeing angels today," he said.

"Messenger angels. Pick up the rose."

He knelt and opened the note attached to the flower stem. *The dragon is slain,* it said.

His smile outdid the sun as he looked up again. "Amy?"

She nodded her head vigorously. "Yes."

"Stay right there." He ran around the building and burst through the front door, then bounded up the stairs two at a time.

Amy's apartment door was unlocked. He pushed it open and walked into bedlam. Hortense swung from the chandelier, Herman whizzed around the room, and the latest invention had gone crazy. Popcorn was spewing into the air and blanketing the floor.

Todd didn't notice a thing except Amy. He waded through the popcorn and took her into his arms.

"I love you, Amy Logan."

"And I love you, Judge Todd Cunningham. Now and for always."

He hugged her close and tipped her face up. "If you hadn't sent that rose flying out your window today, I was going to storm your castle and take you by force tonight."

"I thought of tossing the window box. Aunt Syl talked me out of that before she left for the movie."

"I'm glad she did."

"Of course, there was another consideration."

"What's that, love?"

"I didn't want to crush the father of all my children."

"All? That sounds ominous."

"It is. I want at least six."

"Then I have a wonderful suggestion."

"What?"

"I suggest we get started."

And they did. Right in the middle of the popcorn.

Epilogue

"Hand Mommy that hammer, William. There's a sweetheart. Chad, take that feather out of Baby Sylvia's mouth. Margaret, be a love and stop pulling Hortense's tail."

Amy was hard at work on another invention, but she paused to look lovingly around the sunshiny room at her children. They had already outgrown one house, and if she had her way, they were going to outgrow this one.

"You have that look again, dear." Aunt Syl spoke from a rocking chair beside the window. Time had added a few lines to her face, but it had done nothing to dim her spirit. At eighty she was still turning out best-selling mystery novels.

"What look, Aunt Syl?"

"The look that tells me I should start crocheting bootees."

Amy laughed. "You can't even crochet."

"It's never too late to learn."

"My sentiments exactly." Todd spoke from the doorway. At the sound of his voice, the entire family descended on him. He dispensed kisses and hugs all around and counted himself to be the world's luckiest man.

That night he presided over the family dinner, listened to a recap of everybody's day, and shared the bathing and tucking-in and telling-bedtime-stories chores.

At last he was alone with Amy.

"Come here, Mrs. Cunningham." He spread his arms wide. Amy walked across their bedroom and cuddled against him. He bent down and captured her lips. "I've been wanting to do this all day," he murmured.

"Guess what I've been wanting to do all day?"

"What?"

She stood on tiptoe and whispered into his ear.

A delighted grin split his face. "The last time we did that your bed played 'Dixie,' ". he said.

She leaned back in his arms and slowly began unbuttoning her blouse. "Perhaps we should tell the children." Her silk blouse made a rose-colored splash against the carpet.

"Tell them what?"

"That 'Dixie' isn't a love song." She freed her breasts from their lacy restraint.

Todd lowered his head and took one taut nipple into his mouth. "What a shocking thing to say, Mrs. Cunningham," he murmured against her satin flesh. " 'Dixie' happens to be the only love song I know." He unfastened her skirt.

"Then, Judge Cunningham, I have a suggestion."

"What?" Her skirt hit the floor.

"I suggest you hurry. The bed's playing our song."

THE EDITOR'S CORNER

We have Valentine's Day presents galore for you next month . . . hearts, flowers, chuckles, and a sentimental tear or two. We haven't wrapped your presents in the traditional colors of the special holiday for lovers, though. Rather, we're presenting them in a spectrum of wonderful earth colors from vibrant, exhilarating Green to sinfully rich chocolate Brown. (Apologies to Billie and Sandra for using their last names this way, but I couldn't resist!)

First, in **MAKIN' WHOOPEE,** LOVESWEPT #182, by—of course—Billie Green, you'll discover the perfect Valentine's Day heroine, Sara Love. Ms. Love's business partner (and sweet nemesis) is the wickedly good-looking Charlie Sanderson. These two charmers have been waging a long silent battle to repress their true feelings for one another. He has built for himself a reputation as "Good Time Charlie," the swinging bachelor; she has built walls around her emotions, pouring all her energies into the business. An ill-fated trip to inspect a piece of property is the catalyst for the erosion of their defenses, but it isn't until a little bundle of joy makes an astonishing appearance that these two humorous and heartwarming and sexy people come together at last . . . and forever. With all the freshness, optimism, and excitement we associate with the green of springtime, Billie creates in **MAKIN' WHOOPEE** two characters whose love story you'll long remember.

TANGLES, LOVESWEPT #183, by Barbara Boswell, is a story that dazzled me so much I see it as painted in brilliant yellows and golds. Barbara's heroine, Krista Conway, is a highpowered divorce lawyer who is as beautiful as she is brainy. And to hero Logan Moore, the new judge who is trying Krista's case, she is the most seductive lady he's ever laid eyes on. Now Krista may appear hard as nails, but beneath her beautiful and sophisticated exterior is a

(continued)

tender woman who yearns for a man to love and a family to care for. Logan is one heck of a sexy widower with three delightful children . . . and he's a man who is badly misled by Krista's image and wildly confused by his compelling need for her. In a series of events that by turns sizzle with love and romance and sear with emotional intensity, the **TANGLES** these two wonderful people find themselves in begin to unravel to an unexpectedly beautiful ending. Bravo, Barbara Boswell!

The warm earth colors of orange, pale to dusky, had to have been on the palette of Anne and Ed Kolaczyk as they created **SULTRY NIGHTS,** LOVE-SWEPT #184. In this poignant romance of love lost and love regained, we encounter Rachel Anders years after her passionate affair with Ben Healey. One brilliant, erotic, tenderly emotional summer was all Rachel and Ben had together before he had to leave town. Rachel lived on in pained loss, faced with Ben's silence, and comforted only by the legacy of their passion, a beloved daughter. When they meet again, the attraction between them is fired to even greater heat than they'd known in their youth. But Rachel's secret still will come between them until they find their own path to a love that time could not destroy. Ablaze with intensity, **SULTRY NIGHTS** is a captivating love story.

Sandra Brown is a remarkably talented and hard-working author who seems phenomenal to me in the way she keeps topping herself in the creation of one wonderful love story after another. And here comes another of her delectably sensual love stories, **SUNNY CHANDLER'S RETURN,** LOVESWEPT #185. I referred above to "sinfully rich chocolate." I must have written those words because unconsciously I was still under the sway of a very short, but never-to-be forgotten episode in this book involving triple dipped strawberries. (See if you don't delight in that scene as much as I did.) And speaking of people who are

(continued)

phenomenal in topping themselves, I must mention Barbara Alpert who writes all the splendid back cover copy for our LOVESWEPTs. Her description of Sandra's next book is so terrific that I'm going to give you a sneak preview of the back cover copy. Here's what Barbara wrote.

"The whispers began when she entered the ballroom— and every male eye in the place was caught by the breathtakingly lovely spitfire with the slightly shady reputation. Ty Beaumont knew a heartbreaker when he saw one—and also knew that nothing and nobody could keep him from making her his inside a week's time. He'd bet a case of Wild Turkey on it! Sunny heard his devil's voice drawl in her ear, and couldn't help but notice the man was far too handsome for his own good, but his fierce ardor sparked hers, and his "I'll have you naked yet" smile caused a kind of spontaneous combustion that nothing could quench. Private torments had sent both Ty and Sunny racing from the past, but would revealing their dark secrets let them face the future together?"

We think next month offers you a particularly exciting quartet of LOVESWEPTs, and we hope you enjoy each one immensely.

With every good wish,

Carolyn Nichols

Carolyn Nichols
   Editor
LOVESWEPT
Bantam Books, Inc.
666 Fifth Avenue
New York, NY 10103